ANNA SPARROWS

Asher's Answer

Littles & Lace Book 1

Cover Design by: Ky at Blue Brolli Graphics

First edition

This book was professionally typeset on Reedsy.
Find out more at reedsy.com

For everyone who has ever felt weird or abnormal.
Fuck the haters. You're perfect as you are.

Contents

Preface	ii
Chapter One – Asher	1
Chapter Two – Charlie	6
Chapter Three – Asher	10
Chapter Four – Charlie	18
Chapter Five – Asher	25
Chapter Six – Charlie	37
Chapter Seven – Asher	45
Chapter Eight – Charlie	60
Chapter Nine – Asher	69
Chapter Ten – Charlie	80
Chapter Eleven – Asher	86
Chapter Twelve – Charlie	95
Chapter Thirteen – Asher	105
Chapter Fourteen – Charlie	124
Chapter Fifteen – Asher	127
Chapter Sixteen – Charlie	136
Chapter Seventeen – Asher	146
Chapter Eighteen – Charlie	154
Chapter Nineteen – Asher	161
Epilogue – Charlie	168
Matteo's Mettle - Sneak Peek	175
About the Author	185
Also by Anna Sparrows	187

Preface

While this is a low-angst, sweet & cute romance, this book contains mentions of homophobia, domestic abuse, gun violence, anxiety and panic attacks. It is still a work of fiction, though, so some suspension of disbelief may also be necessary with regards to the trajectory of Charlie's career. Apologies in advance if my cursory research into policing appears informed by pop-culture more than real situations.

Also, please bear in mind that this book is an MM Age Play/Age Regression romance between consenting adults and **does** include ABDL and wetting. I am a firm believer in not yucking someone else's yum, so if this kink squicks you, don't read it. Life's too short to read something you don't enjoy.

Chapter One – Asher

What's more humiliating than being kicked out of home by your already homophobic father because he opened your private delivery to discover the adult-sized diapers, onesies, and pacifier you'd bought yourself on a drunken whim? Turning up to your boyfriend's place with your rolling suitcase filled with the only possessions you could gather in ten minutes, only to find him balls deep in someone else.

Someone with breasts and a vagina.

"So, Ash," Cooper says, rubbing the back of his neck awkwardly, as though I didn't just drop my bags and loudly interrupt him midcoitus. "This...thing...between you and me? Kind of more experimental than anything, y'know?"

No. No, I didn't know. But I sure as shit do now.

I open my mouth to tell him that bisexuality and pansexuality are each valid parts of the spectrum, but close it when I realize that, even so, I just caught the asshole cheating on me.

How'd I miss the signs?

"I…" I have no idea what I actually want to say. His new lover chooses this moment to saunter across the hallway behind him, from the bedroom into the bathroom. Buck naked. Objectively, I can see she's hot, even if I'm not interested in women. All blonde hair to her waist and hourglass curves. Feminine in all the ways I'm masculine. I sigh and give up whatever fight was left in me. "Okay. Yeah. Whatever."

That's me, Asher Scanlon: pacifist, submissive, and complete, utter coward.

Coop's gray-blue eyes fill with relief.

Should it hurt more that we're over? It probably should. Honestly, though, I'm more upset that he was my last option for a place to stay. Being an unemployed student with zero social life (because I've let Cooper dominate all aspects of my life for the last year) has left me without a backup plan. Somehow, I don't think any of his buddies —who he's spent months trying to convince me are totally my friends too, even though they barely acknowledge my existence— are going to let me couch surf at their places, either.

"You're the best, Ash." Cooper slugs me in the shoulder all bro-style.

That's what the last year has been reduced to. Ugh.

Then he looks down at the suitcase and duffel I'd dropped when I'd walked in on him and…what was her name? Bethany? Bianca? He kind of introduced her during the awkward 'What is going on?' portion of the evening. And yeah, alright, her name doesn't matter. I'm just trying to distract myself from the inevitable.

Cooper's reddish-brown eyebrows furrow as he looks at my meager possessions. "The hell?" He looks back up at me. "What's with the bags?"

An hour ago, I would have fallen into his arms and sobbed out the whole sorry story, screw my embarrassment over my secret interests. But he's not my person anymore, and even though my throat is tight with emotion, I manage to hold back my breakdown. "Dad kicked me out," I tell him with a shrug. "I was planning to crash here, but—"

"Coop, are you going to fuck me properly or not?"

I can't help snorting at the classy interruption. "For obvious reasons, I think that's a bad idea." I finish, gesturing toward the bathroom.

Cooper, at least, has the decency to appear apologetic. "Shit. Asher, I'm sorry." He hesitates, then offers, "You can take the couch?"

"Honestly?" I bend down and pick up my bags, shaking my head. "I'd rather cut off my dick with a rusty spoon at this point." With what little dignity I have left after my hellish afternoon, I straighten my shoulders and jut my chin toward the bathroom. "Good luck with that."

Then I leave his place, haul my bags back into the trunk of my beaten-up old sedan, and rest my head on my steering wheel.

"What the actual fuck do I do now?"

* * *

I wind up parking my car in one of the parking structures on the college campus. I've got two weeks left on my monthly parking permit, though I know Campus Security does frequent sweeps and if I'm caught living in my car that'll only end badly. Instead, I grab the backpack I keep in the back seat and fill it with a few necessities from my hastily packed luggage, including my laptop and its charger, and make my way toward the library, recalling that it's open twenty-four hours to cater to students' random schedules.

It's not the best plan in the world, but it's the only one I've come up with. I can pretend to have fallen asleep studying if I get caught sleeping on one of the inviting giant beanbags in a reading nook. The stress of the day has my Little side simmering just beneath the surface and I employ every trick in the book to keep Little Ash from making an appearance.

I've been able to keep this side of me well hidden —indulging in Little play and regressing only when I've been completely alone— and I have no intention of slipping publicly. Hell, not even Cooper knows about my interest in the BDSM lifestyle, and I'm more relieved about that now than ever. Sometimes I worry that he suspects some of my kinks. I might have slipped and called him Daddy in the bedroom a time or two. But he's never said anything. He might be a cheater, and incredibly selfish, but he isn't a horrible person.

Or maybe I'm just that starved for affection.

Either way, it's been too long since the last time I allowed myself to enter my Little headspace and I'm terrified that, with the additional stress of suddenly being homeless and without any support, I'm going to snap and drop into it without meaning or wanting to. As much as I enjoy giving up control, I want to be able to manage when I do. It has to be on my terms. Unfortunately, when I'm particularly anxious, that's not always possible.

"Suck it up, Scanlon," I mutter to myself as I trudge toward the library's reading nook, hoping that hearing the words out loud might trick me into believing they're coming from a Daddy or a Dom. "Gotta be a big boy right now."

It's late in the evening and there's nobody else around to

hear my deranged murmurings, which is a good thing because I don't know that I could fight off the embarrassment of anyone hearing that. Of them potentially working out my secret.

As I finally sink into the welcoming embrace of cotton-covered polystyrene balls with my laptop perched on my thighs, I begin to relax. I've got a laundry list of things I need to work out. I need to find a place to live, which means finding a job, which probably means dropping out of college. I can't afford school now anyway — Dad made that crystal clear when he told me I was out on my ass and cut off completely.

A sob threatens to tear its way from the back of my throat, but I bite down on my clenched fist and hold it back through sheer willpower. I refuse to cry over anything that man said to me.

Dropping out isn't the worst thing that could happen, I tell myself after taking deep, meditative breaths. *I hate college anyway.*

I was only doing the damn business degree to shut my father up. So what if I've only got a semester left? It's not as though I was going to use the degree, is it?

At twenty-two, I should probably have a better idea of what I do want to do with my life, but I'm spiraling right now, so thinking beyond getting myself through the next few days isn't possible.

I spend the next couple of hours applying for jobs online —everything from simple cashier positions to administrative support— and then start scrolling real estate listings for anyone in search of a roommate within my extremely limited budget. My eyes grow heavy as I read listing after listing, and soon enough I'm drifting into oblivion.

Chapter Two – Charlie

"So then I told the punk to beat it before I went full Dom on his ass and... You're not even listening, are you?"

I shake my head and turn to my younger brother, an apology already on the tip of my tongue. His dark-brown eyes narrow at me and he lobs a fry from his plate across the table in our dingy station lunchroom. It hits me in the chest and I scowl, trying to brush off the tiny dot of grease it left on the light-blue material. "Asshole." I huff. "Was that necessary?"

"Charlie, you weren't listening to me," he whines.

I roll my eyes. "Yeah, you're *really* selling the Dom vibes, Josh."

Josh scoffs, but a smile is tugging at his lips. He's as far from a Dom as anyone can get, and we both know it. Still, to look at him you wouldn't guess he's actually a pretty adorable sub.

We're both cops, with him fairly new to the force, having graduated from the Academy last year, and we both like our gym time. At six foot three, I eclipse his height by about two inches, but he's broader across the chest than I am. His eyes are dark where mine are blue, but we both sport the same dark hair and stubble across our matching jawlines.

But that's where the similarities end. Even though there's eight years of age between us, we have a close enough relationship that we're aware of each other's kinks. In fact, he can thank me for introducing him to the world of age play where we've both found our niche.

"Speaking of," he asks, "you gonna check out The Grove with me tonight?"

We're both rostered off for the next couple of days, and it's been a long time since either of us saw any action. He's predominantly a scene Little, while I'm a mostly lifestyle Daddy.

After my last breakup, I've been questioning whether the right boy is out there for me. I'm looking for someone whose Little side is more fluid, who doesn't mind that my job is unpredictable and that the hours mean that a rigid schedule is impossible for me to uphold. I need someone who connects with me, not only as a Daddy when they're Little but also as a partner and a lover when they're Big. An equal, I guess. I don't mind being a caregiver, but I don't want it to be a twenty-four-seven thing. But I don't just want scheduled scene play, either. I'm fussy like that.

It all feels a bit like a pipe dream at this point. Maybe hitting up The Grove —a club which caters to all aspects of the BDSM community, located on the fringe of the city— isn't a bad idea. If nothing else, spoiling a boy rotten for a night will be more relaxing than heading home to jerk off to porn.

"You meeting someone specific there?" I ask Josh, smirking because he's a bit of a brat and has chased off the last couple of Daddies he's played with. I've never tried to fill that role for my baby brother because it just feels weird, since I usually equate the lifestyle with my sexual relationships. But I've still got a setup at my place with all the kiddie comforts he could need for emergency Little time just in case. He's never had to use it, but the unspoken offer is there. He's currently living with our parents, so there's no chance for him to indulge at home.

He rolls his eyes. "Nah. After Declan, I'm taking a break. But it's been a while and" —he rolls his neck and shoulders— "I'm getting antsy to let go, y'know?"

"I get it," I assure him gently. Because, yeah, I do. The last few months without a boy in my life have been difficult. I genuinely like having someone to care for, even without the sex. (But, Christ, I miss the sex, too.) Checking my watch, I offer, "My shift's over at five. Should we meet there around eight?" It gives me time to shower, change, and have dinner.

"Sounds good." Josh stands and balls up the remains of his take-out meal. He checks his own watch and exhales. "I've gotta get back to it. I'll see you there." My partner, Max, nods at him as they cross paths on Josh's way out of the break room.

Even though we work in the same precinct, Josh and I are on different teams. It's not often we get the chance to meet for lunch, but it's been a slow week. The city's not exactly a criminal hotspot, not any worse than other cities in the country, but we still have to deal with our share of break-ins, assaults, and domestic violence.

With Josh still green, he's got an easy beat to walk over by the college campus downtown. Max and I cover the shadier areas in the city proper. Our arrests generally happen after dark, though some of the local dealers have been brazenly conducting their business in daylight lately. More often than not, we respond to calls and do footwork for the detectives in the precinct. It works for me.

"Josh looks good," Max observes with a grin as I toss my own shit into a waiting trash can. He's a handful of years older than me and has been my partner for the past three years. He knows just how anxious I was about my kid brother joining the force.

I nudge his shoulder with my own. "Yeah, turns out he's a natural." As far as I'm aware, Max doesn't know anything about our kinkier lives, but I've previously confessed my concerns that Josh's naturally more submissive nature had me worried at his choice of career. But it turns out it helps with talking to people; getting witness statements and talking people down from volatile situations are kind of his forte.

"He looks up to you, Charlie." Max bobs his head, a lock of blond hair falling across his eyes. He blows it back. "It's cute."

I can't help laughing. "Don't ever call him cute to his face. You'll live to regret it."

Then we're out of the building, climbing into our patrol car, and our conversation turns to other things.

Chapter Three — Asher

I stare with wide eyes at the cop in front of me, willing myself to not burst into tears. I've managed to get away with my plan of essentially living on campus for four days, but the Campus Security guy must have gotten suspicious after seeing me asleep in the same place three nights in a row. I've been showering in the on-campus gym and living off packets of instant ramen, rationing what little money I have because I still haven't found a job.

The tall, buff police officer who came to investigate Security's call has me wanting my blankie and binkie But *that* would only get me thrown into the psych ward at this point, so I try to paste on a winning smile and convince the guy —"Officer J. Walker" his name tag reads, and I do my best not to crack a jaywalking joke because I'm sure he's heard it before— that it's all a misunderstanding.

"P-please," I tell him, hating the shakiness of my voice. "I've just b-been researching late, a-and it's all totally aboveboard." My voice has pitched higher and my thumb has inched toward my mouth. I suck on it briefly, then catch myself and withhold a groan. Unable to completely remove it, I bite down on it and hope the cop thinks it's just an anxious tic. "I didn't mean to do a-anything wrong."

Because I'm a good boy. I swear it. I'm a very good boy. These words almost leave my lips and I bite down harder on the tip of my thumb to prevent it from happening.

Oh, God, no. Not now. I force my thumb back out of my mouth and clench my jaw tight. *I am an adult.*

"Hey, it's okay." The cop's tone is low and soothing, and he reaches out to steady me. His dark eyes are warm and with the way they flicker to my thumb, awkwardly hovering near my lips, they light with understanding. *Fuck.* "Asher, right?" I nod, and he continues. "Asher, breathe for me, buddy."

He leads me out of the library, shouldering my backpack and guiding me with a hand between my shoulder blades. "We're just gonna sit out here in the sunshine and have a chat, okay?"

I can't get arrested. I can't. I wasn't hurting anyone.

If I get arrested, who's going to want to hire me? Who'll let me rent a room?

"Nobody's arresting anyone," he assures me as he leads me over to a bench near the front gardens of the campus. I can feel the burn of a blush on my cheeks.

"I said that out loud, huh?"

The policeman's lips quirk. "You did. I'd say you're stressing out more than you realize." He drops my bag onto the seat between us and reaches for the zipper. "I'm guessing you've got a blanket or stuffie or something in here that'll help with that."

My lower lip wobbles because, yeah, I do, and fuck him for knowing that. I feel vulnerable and exposed and embarrassed.

"I… I can't…" My gaze darts around, keenly aware that I'm drawing curious stares from passersby. Or maybe it's the attractive man in the uniform who is doing his level best to talk me down from an anxiety attack. Either way, I don't need people seeing. I certainly don't want people knowing.

"Is there anyone I can call for you?" He lowers his voice and tries to look me in the eye. "A Daddy or a Mommy?"

Damn it, he really does know. Is it that obvious?

"No…no one," I manage to get out before my voice breaks. I feel myself slip a little further. "No. No Daddy." Then I'm hyperventilating because, fuck, I wish I did have a Daddy. I wouldn't be in this mess if I did. I'd have someone to stay with. Someone to care for me. And I wouldn't have to hide this part of me. Not all the time. Maybe not ever. But that's just a dream, and it'll never happen.

I don't have the guts to go looking for a Daddy. I haven't even been brave enough to anonymously join an online group, and the idea of seeking out a local munch petrifies me.

As far as I'm concerned, I do have to hide this side of me, and I am alone, and I'm scared. I'm terrified, actually.

Why can't I be normal?

"Asher, breathe," the officer commands gently, and I try. I really do. But my hands are shaking, and the stress of the last few days is building, and the tears are coming…and I can't stop any of it.

"Okay, new plan," he decides, lifting my bag back to his shoulder as he stands and lightly pulls me up by my bicep. "We're going to go for a drive, okay? And, no, you're not under arrest. Don't panic."

Except then I'm being guided into the back of a freaking police car and he's murmuring with his partner, an older lady who keeps shooting me concerned looks through the rearview mirror. She reverses the car out onto the street while he pulls out his phone and calls someone, pitching his voice low as he talks; but he turns in his seat and keeps his dark-brown eyes on me.

I hang my head in shame and let the tears roll down my cheeks. At least I'm not sobbing.

I hadn't thought things could get more embarrassing than they were at the beginning of the week, but I'd been wrong.

* * *

I must have fallen asleep during the drive, because I'm gently being shaken awake by another cop. He looks a lot like Officer Jaywalker, but his eyes are a deep shade of blue and have a couple of laugh lines in their corners where Jaywalker does not. Also I can't help noticing that his scruff is thicker and darker, and I have the urge to rub my cheek across his jaw like a cat.

What the actual fuck is wrong with me?

"Hey, bud," this cop croons, smiling at me with what feels like genuine warmth. "You're safe, okay? And definitely not under arrest."

"Well, that's something," I say with a sigh, closing my eyes and shaking my head. I can see the original cop lurking behind this one on the other side of the open car door.

"So, my name's Charlie," this new cop tells me with the same warm tone that should not be sending happy vibes to my Little self. I try to push that headspace further away even as Charlie leans over me and unbuckles my belt for me in a classic Daddy move. "And I think we should go inside and have a chat, okay?"

I panic at the thought of having to go into a freaking police station, but as Charlie takes my hand and helps me out of the car, I frown in confusion at the house in front of me. "What… Where are we?" The original officer hands me my backpack and, despite myself, I cuddle it in front of me like a plush toy.

"My house," Charlie says calmly, as though it's perfectly normal for police officers to go rogue and bring young guys on the brink of a meltdown to their personal homes. He nods his head at the cop that looks like him and adds, "Thanks, Josh. I've got him from here."

Wait. Hold up. I'm being left here with this new guy all alone? Nope. This is how serial killer movies start.

The thought is such a valid one, in fact, that I stamp my foot and repeat it aloud.

Charlie chuckles and shakes his head, and Josh —who I've decided I will forever call Jaywalker out of spite— pats me on the shoulder and assures me, "It's okay, Ash. I promise. Charlie's going to look after you. He's good at that." Before I can read too deeply into the statement, Josh closes the rear car door and climbs back into the passenger seat gracefully. The window slides down and he says, "I'll see you later," before the car pulls away from the curb. It's then that I notice a second car —a sleek, black, later-model SUV— parked in the driveway.

"C'mon, Asher." Charlie coaxes me forward to the clapboard home.

It's two stories, painted gray with white accents, with a wraparound porch. It's got a cute cottage feel about it. Welcoming and homey.

Just the sort of façade a serial killer wants you to see.

"I'm not a serial killer." Charlie laughs, and once again I realize I've spoken my thoughts out loud. "And I know this is unorthodox, but Josh said you've been sleeping in the library on campus and that you panicked and lapsed into Little space when he got there to talk to you..." He turns and frowns at me, because the second he mentioned "Little space" I froze. "Shit." He bounds back down the three front stairs and takes my hand in his. This action feels better than it has a right to. "Come on, baby. Inside. We'll talk."

Baby.

Nobody's ever called me baby. Not even Cooper. It's a generic endearment, but it feels like fireworks have exploded inside me. My heart hammers and my head feels fuzzy, and Little Ash comes hurtling back to the surface.

"'Kay," I respond, allowing him to tug me up the front stairs of his picturesque house and into the little foyer.

Inside is just as pretty as outside. It's all polished timber floors and white walls with French provincial-style furnishings. Painted white surfaces, golden-hued wood, and gray linens. The whole thing is like something straight out of a magazine. It's almost incongruous with the very manly police officer who apparently lives here.

Maybe the decorating is his wife's doing?

I don't like that thought, and I don't want to analyze why very closely.

I'm still clutching my backpack, but soon enough Charlie's in front of me, easing it out of my tight grip.

"We're just gonna put this down here," he tells me, setting it on the floor inside the doorway before opening the zipper and digging around inside the bag. He pulls out my blankie —a faded green fleece decorated with bunnies— and my binkie, holding both out to me. I take them with shaking hands, my cheeks on fire.

Nobody else has ever seen these items, let alone touched

them, but he's just handing them over as though this is totally normal.

"Juice?" he asks me while he gently guides me through the open-plan living and dining areas and into the kitchen at the back of the house. It's a U-shaped kitchen with gleaming appliances and a large central island with three high-backed stools set in front of it. So far, there's no sign of a wife. I'm not relieved. I'm not. "Or milk, or water?"

"Juice, please," I answer and bring my blankie up to my face. I stroke the corner against my cheek, trying to calm my racing heart as a sippy cup is carefully slid in front of me. I inhale sharply.

"It's okay," Charlie repeats in that deep, low voice that has *Daddy* written all over it. Even if I have had zero experience with Daddies to this point, I can't help but feel like I'm reading him correctly on this. Plus, you know, the sippy gives him away. He nudges the cup. "Go on, you can drink it."

I'm a little overwhelmed by how open and accepting this simple action is. Additionally, it's been so long since I allowed myself a chance to be Little that, when I pick the cup up, I smother another sob.

"Hey." Before I know it, I'm being held against an incredibly firm chest and a large, masculine hand is carding through the mop of curls on my head. "It's alright, baby. It's okay."

I'm not exactly a small guy. I'm five foot eleven, and I've worked hard to bulk up since my teens. But cradled by this man, I feel Little...and unexpectedly cared for. How is that possible when we've only just met? It's not a bad feeling, but it makes me instantly more vulnerable and a touch confused.

The last vestiges of my resolve break, and the tears I shed in the back of Josh's car are nothing in comparison to the meltdown I have now. But Charlie holds me through it all, through the snot and the tears and the heaving, body-wracking cries, soothing and rocking me until I've exhausted myself.

Then he helps me lift the cup to my lips, encouraging me to drink, and I do.

Chapter Four — Charlie

When Josh texted me near the end of my shift with his concerns about a kid who'd been caught living in the campus library, I wasn't quite sure what to expect. The follow-up phone call informed me that the kid had panicked, slipped into a Little headspace, and didn't seem to have anyone to support him; it also cinched my resolve to help, even if only for one night. If nothing else, I'd help my brother with his job. I had a particular set of skills and experiences that could help in this situation, after all.

Then he and his partner, Samara, had pulled up with the kid asleep in the back seat. I chatted briefly with them about the situation and Sam leveled me with a knowing look, even though I know Josh wouldn't have told her anything about my personal life. She's an observant cop and a smart woman. Having watched the kid in the backseat interact with Josh before he told her that I had a unique perspective that could help, she's surely put two and two together.

It doesn't bother me. I'm not ashamed of my preferences

or my kinks, especially when my desire is to live the lifestyle and not just play temporary scenes. I've always known that, sooner or later, my personal and private lives were going to intersect. As long as it doesn't impact my ability to do my job, my colleagues shouldn't care.

The kid, though. God, he's adorable. He's got wide hazel eyes, a mop of chestnut-colored curls on his head, and an athletic build, with broad shoulders that taper down to slim hips and strong thighs. He's perfection, and from the moment I saw him, the desire to hold and protect and look after him fired along my synapses.

Don't rush this, I remind myself. *The poor kid will need you to go slow.* Josh said Asher was shaken and flighty, and apparently terrified of admitting he indulges in Little play for comfort.

Considering Josh's observations, Asher's breakdown in my kitchen should not have surprised me, but his cries twist something inside me. I'm a Daddy through and through. Holding him as he sobs is heart-wrenching, even though it feels so good to step back into this role. It will be difficult to hold back and pace myself with this boy, especially when I can see how desperately he needs someone to care for him.

He finally exhausts himself and I get him to drink from the cup that seems to have set this whole thing off. He sags against me, and I'm filled with so much warmth that it takes me a moment to get my bearings.

"Okay, baby," I murmur, and I just can't resist dusting my lips over the top of his head. The endearment comes naturally around him —he's so much softer and more fragile than a simple 'boy'— but he hasn't protested my use of the word the few times it has slipped out already. I need to rein my enthusiasm in, but rational thought is failing me.

Asher sighs and snuggles into my chest, and I'm officially a goner. Five fucking minutes alone with this kid, and I'm wrapped around his little finger. I can't even pretend that it's not happening. Josh will be insanely proud of himself when he checks in later: he would have taken one look at Ash and pegged him as my type. He knows me too well, and as I rub my hand over Ash's back, I can't bring myself to be bothered by that. In fact, I want to thank my brother. *God, I'm such a sap.*

"Come on." I tenderly urge the boy in my arms to stand. "Let's clean up your face and get comfy, okay?"

He's pliant now. I want to praise him for being so brave and for knowing that, usually, being led into a stranger's house can be unsafe…but now's not the time for that conversation. No, he's too far gone, too wrung out and lost in his head, and I'm going to care for him until he's Big again. Only then will we talk about the bigger issues at hand.

I lead him back through the living area and up the stairs that start near the foyer. Up here, there are three bedrooms as well as two bathrooms: the main bathroom and the ensuite, which is attached to the primary bedroom. At the top of the stairs, I head straight for the main bathroom and sit him gently on the edge of the tub. His gaze scans the space, and he blinks when he notices the basket of bath toys, but he doesn't say a word. I'm sure he's worked out by now that I'm a Daddy.

I pull a bright-blue washcloth from the cupboard beneath the sink and run the faucet until the water is warm. Then I wet the cloth, wring it out, and wipe over Asher's face, clearing it of the dried tears and snot.

"Thank you," he murmurs, so quietly that I almost miss it.

"My pleasure, baby," I tell him, then take his hand and head back out into the small living area that connects all the rooms.

"I've gotta change my shirt," I explain, leading him toward the couch, "but I'll be right back."

There's a small TV up here, and I consider offering to put on some cartoons, but I am only going to be a minute or two at most, and he's not exactly in the right mindset to focus on anything. What he needs is a nap; I hesitate, wanting to ask him if he needs to be diapered beforehand, but I can tell that to ask as much would tip him over the edge again. If seeing a sippy cup was enough to break him, I'm certain a diaper would be too much to handle right now.

I make quick work of changing out of my uniform shirt in favor of a soft green T-shirt, and I return to the boy on my couch with haste.

"Okay, bud. Nap time."

He blinks up at me owlishly, as though trying to process the words.

"You're drained," I tell him, dropping to a crouch in front of him. "You've had a big day. A nap will help you feel better."

"Yeah..." he says with a slow nod. He's not quite in Little space, but he's certainly not with me as an adult, either.

"Do you need to potty first?"

The question snaps him to attention and his cheeks flush. "Uh...yeah."

"Do you need help?"

Asher shakes his head quickly, the blush in his cheeks deepening. "No." But there's *something* in his gaze that tells me this isn't a hard limit for him. Almost like embarrassment and curiosity melding together: a simmering enthusiasm he can't quite stifle in time.

Interesting.

"Okay," I say, not pushing the issue. I lead him back to the main bathroom. "Do your thing, wash your hands, and then I'll show you your room."

"My room?" he echoes, hovering in the doorway of the bathroom.

I nod and can't resist swatting at his cute little ass. "Potty first. Scoot." I barely remember to grab his blankie from his hand before he carries it in there with him.

Asher has the presence of mind to close the door, and it's not long before I hear the toilet flush and the faucet run. He opens the door, his eyes much sharper than they were before he headed into the bathroom. "You don't have to do this," he says. "And I'm sorry to have put you through" —he makes a vague hand gesture between us as his cheeks turn adorably pink again— "everything."

Cocking an eyebrow, I reach out and hold his chin between my thumb and index finger, tilting his head up to look at me. "I want to do this, Asher. And we're going to talk it all through. But I honestly think you should have a nap first." I keep my voice low but firm. "Would you be more comfortable talking now, or after a nap?"

His eyes dart from side to side as they look into mine, and I can tell he's gauging my resolve. There's spirit inside this kid, and I suspect that once he's comfortable he'll be a lot of fun. On a shaky inhale, he grudgingly admits, "After a nap."

"Good boy." I'm not oblivious to the shiver these words of praise send through him. Letting go of his chin, I press a kiss to his forehead, delighting in the renewed blush it causes, and take his hand in mine again. "Come on. Let's see your room."

I hand him back his blankie and take him to the bedroom on the far side of the stairs, the one just on the other side of the living space from the primary suite. When I open the door,

I try to see the space from an outsider's perspective. It's big enough to house a queen-size bed with two bedside tables comfortably, but there's also a low-lying bookshelf which is covered in kids' books, a few plush toys, and a little set of Duplo bricks currently built into a castle shape. The bed's quilt cover has splashes of primary colors against a white backdrop, and the lamps on either side of the bed look like they've been built from Lego blocks.

"Oh," Asher breathes as he steps into the space, and I watch as his eyes go round and shiny. "Wow."

"You like it?" I know he does. It's warm and welcoming and perfect for a little boy, but I want to hear him say it.

He swallows roughly and nods. "It's amazing."

The walls are painted a pale blue with fluffy white clouds scattered abstractly. The carpet is a deep shade of blue and is lush and thick beneath our feet. In the built-in cupboard, I have a selection of onesies and pajamas which should fit him, as well as new pairs of training pants and some diapers...but they can all wait for another time.

And yeah, I'm honestly that hooked on this boy already. I don't care how insane that sounds. He's clearly uncertain and vulnerable, but if Josh is right and Asher doesn't have anyone? I want to be his someone. Well, I want to try. At the very least, I want to help him get back on his feet. I'm not letting this beautiful boy become another statistic.

"I'm glad you think so," I reply to his assessment, unable to hide my pride. "It's yours for as long as you want it."

He pins those wide hazel eyes on me in surprise. "*What*? You don't even know me. I—"

"Shh." Smoothing my hand through his curls, I shake my head. "We'll talk after your nap, I promise."

Asher makes a strangled sound at the back of his throat, his disbelief more than obvious. However, it doesn't stop him from cautiously inching toward the bed. I take the lead, pulling back the covers and gesturing for him to climb up; then I slide in beside him and pull him close, until his head is resting on my chest. I remember that I picked his pacifier up from the kitchen bench after his crying jag, and I pull it from my pocket and offer it to him. After a brief moment of hesitation, he takes it. He casts me another careful look from under his long lashes before he pops the pacifier into his mouth, and my heart squeezes.

Usually, I'd offer to read a book, but he's not entirely Little and I think just getting him used to my presence is enough for now.

Behind the rhythmic sucking sound, Asher's breathing evens out within fifteen minutes, and it takes a handful more for me to gently pull away. I help him out of his socks and shoes and watch him for a few more seconds before I force myself to walk out the door.

Chapter Five — Asher

I t's dark when I wake up, and I blink as my eyes adjust to the dim light filtering through the window of the strange room.

It takes me longer than I'd like for the day's events to click into place in my brain; but when they do, I leap out of the sinfully comfortable bed and pause as my bare feet hit the carpet. My Binky drops from my mouth and hits the plush blue surface with a dull thud. I scoop it up and shove it into my hip pocket, wiggling my toes.

Charlie must have removed my shoes and socks while I napped.

He's such a Daddy, my brain helpfully supplies, and I fight the urge to groan. Despite my earlier meltdown at college, I don't need a Daddy. Adding additional complications to my life right now would not be a smart move. Especially when I've never explored this aspect of my life with anyone else. I'm not ready.

Except this entire afternoon did feel magical.

From being held and rocked, to the kisses on my forehead...
hell, even the embarrassing potty talk. It's all I've ever dreamed
about. Plus, he has toys and a huge bathtub and coloring books
and kids' books to read and...it's all too good to be true. As if a
man as insanely attractive and perfect as Charlie would want
to be *my* Daddy. I'm too unpredictable. Too inexperienced
with this kink. I've only read a little bit online, after all: just
enough to experiment with being Little on my own. I'm too
ashamed —too broken and anxious, even— to be a good Little
for someone else.

I find my shoes and socks tucked neatly away in front of
the door and pick them up, snag my blankie off the bed, then
quietly pad across the small living area and down the stairs.
I just make it to the front door and lift my backpack when
Charlie's deep voice stops me. He speaks with firm finality,
demanding attention. "*Asher.*"

My shoulders drop in resignation, and I turn to face him,
feeling guilty for attempting to flee without saying a word. He's
got his arms folded and a frown on his face that tells me he
knows exactly what I was trying to do.

Unable to meet his gaze, I try not to drool over his biceps
because *hot damn* they're something else.

"I was just—"

"Running away?" His tone is dry, but there might be a tiny
bit of amusement in it.

I nod. "I'm sorry. You've been..." I struggle to find the right
words. "...unbelievably good about my whole...well, *me*." I
hang my head. "But I can't stay here."

"I hate to tell you this, kiddo, but you can't live in the library
on campus, either."

I startle at how close he sounds now and when I look up,

26

he's directly in front of me. There's not even a foot of space between us. And, huh, did he smell this delicious earlier? Fuck. *Focus, Ash.*

I try to take a step backward, but I meet a wall of firm muscle and squeal.

"Easy there, bud." The front door is open and the police officer who didn't exactly arrest me but who did put me in the back of his patrol car is standing behind me, his hands up in the universal gesture of surrender. He shoots an amused look over the top of my head. "You still haven't gotten him inside? It's been hours, Charlie."

"Fuck you," Charlie shoots back with a smile. "He's just woken up from a nap. I've been cooking dinner." He looks at me and then the other cop. "Ash, you remember my brother, Josh."

Brothers. Well, that makes sense. They do look very alike, only I guess that Josh is closer to my age and Charlie's a little older than us. Maybe thirty? Not that it matters. I'm not planning on sticking around.

With my heart still beating madly from the surprise of backing into the younger of the two, I glance between them and attempt to charm my way out. "Well, as fun as it's been playing 'Hot Cop, Hotter Cop,' I'm just gonna go now."

"I hope I'm Hotter Cop," Josh says playfully, while Charlie groans and pulls me back via my backpack.

"You're an idiot," Charlie tells his brother, then gives me a gentle shove into the living room. "And you and I have a lot to talk about."

"Do we have to?" I ask, managing to keep the whine from my tone.

"Yes," he answers plainly. I'm guided to the couch, and he

27

sits beside me, turning his body in to face mine until our knees bump.

"Josh, can you keep an eye on the spaghetti sauce?" He directs the question over my shoulder in his brother's direction, and we all hear the dismissal for what it is.

But Josh calls back his agreement, and his footsteps fade away as he heads further into the house.

Then Charlie's blue eyes are on mine again, and he takes my hands in his, as if he's afraid I'm going to run if he doesn't tether me down. To be fair, he's not far off the mark. I send a look of longing in the direction of the front door, but Charlie squeezes my hands, silently demanding my attention again.

"Let's start with the easy stuff first, okay?" he says, and I snort because there's nothing about my situation that's easy. His eyes narrow. "Why were you living in the library? And don't try and tell me that it's all a misunderstanding. Josh said Security has footage of you using the showers in the gym and going back to the library every night for the last week."

"It's only been three nights." I sigh, concluding that the jig is up. "And it's only been while I try to find a new place."

"What happened to your old place?"

I flinch. The wound is still raw, and humiliation thrums through my veins.

"Ash?"

When I look up, his eyes are full of compassion and concern, and that has me talking, even though I really don't want to. "My dad kicked me out. He...well, he opened a package of stuff that he really shouldn't have" —my cheeks burn— "and he flipped out. Called me..." The words aren't ones I want to repeat, burned deep into my psyche, making the shame and embarrassment I already felt ten times worse. "Well, he called me a bunch of names and told me I had ten minutes to pack my essentials and get out."

"Oh, baby." The words are soft, but Charlie's expression pulls into a scowl after he says them. I know the look is intended for my dad, but I pull back from him instinctively. The anger on his face is immediately schooled into sympathy; I don't know if that makes me feel much better. "I'm sorry. Your dad's a dick." He squeezes my hands. "Go on."

"So...I did. And then I went to..."

"To?" He prompts me to continue.

"To my ex's place." My face burns again. "He wasn't exactly my ex until I walked in on him with his new girlfriend. So, fuck me, right?" I feel so stupid all over again. How could I not have seen what Cooper was doing? "And, other than him, I don't have any friends. I'm... I'm not exactly an extrovert, and Cooper kind of dominated my life for the last year..." Likely a tactical move on his part. I'm rational enough to see that now. I don't know how I manage to keep my shit together when I finish by saying, "I didn't have anywhere else to go..."

I'm wrapped in strong arms and breathing in the spicy scent of Charlie's cologne before I know it. I can feel myself trembling, but unlike earlier, I don't fall apart. The nap and my earlier breakdowns have helped me get myself back under control.

"The stuff your dad found..." Charlie begins slowly, still holding me. He can probably feel my heart race as my embarrassment kicks in. "It was kinky stuff, right? *Little* things?"

I can only nod, shame turning my stomach into a lead weight.

Charlie pulls me in tighter and I wind up in his lap with my face pressed into the crook of his neck. It's not an unpleasant place to find myself. And, damn, he really does smell good.

"Sweetheart, there's nothing wrong with being Little, you know that, right?"

His words make my heart sing, but I still feel my face flame and I shake my head. "I'm a freak," I mutter, repeating one of my dad's less disturbing descriptions. I'd already been feeling abnormal, but his bellows of rage had cemented my worries.

"No, baby, you're not."

"Says the hot cop who doesn't wonder what it's like to wear a diaper." My stomach turns to lead again, the words having bypassed my filter entirely.

Jesus fucking Christ, who is in control of my mouth?

Charlie chuckles and rubs my back. "I don't want to wear one, no...but I like changing them."

Dead. I am officially dead. But, before I can say anything, his brother asks, "What about a hot cop that *is* into wearing them occasionally? Am I a freak?"

"*What?*" I squeak, pulling my bright red face away from Charlie long enough to stare across the room at Josh.

He's leaning against the archway that separates the living room from the dining area, casual as you please. He shrugs. "It's not a lifestyle thing for me, but I like to play occasionally." He gestures to Charlie with a jerk of his stubbled chin. "This one's *always* in Daddy mode, but you've probably realized that by now." He cocks his head, gaze flitting back to his brother. "Dinner's good to go, by the way."

Still in a state of shock, I allow Charlie to push me up and lead me to the kitchen with his hand on the small of my back. I glance back and forth between the brothers. Far be it from me to judge, but... "Do you two ever...?"

"No." Charlie's reply is quick and vehement. He helps me

climb up and sit at the middle stool before I even notice, then walks around the kitchen island, gathering plates and cups for dinner. "Nope. He's my brother. That'd be weird because, for me, being a Daddy's always gone hand in hand with my sexual relationships. But," he adds, and I suspect it's more for Josh's benefit than mine, "if he ever needed me to, I'd be his caregiver in an emergency."

Josh smiles back at him softly. "It's appreciated, big brother." Then Josh leans in and nudges me with his shoulder. "So...am I a freak?"

"No!" I frown. "I wouldn't ever think that."

"Cool." He smirks. "So what's the difference? Why's it okay for me and not you?"

"I..." I stop. I don't have an answer to that.

A child-sized melamine bowl of spaghetti with a thick tomato sauce is slid in front of me, and I look across the counter to meet Charlie's sparkling eyes.

"Exactly," he says, then produces a sippy cup of milk. My stomach flip-flops, a strange surge of affection washing over me. His next words only make the feeling stronger. "So now you just have to work on reminding yourself that you're perfect as you are."

* * *

Josh gives me a hug after dinner, then hugs his brother and leaves after saying something about visiting a grove by himself. I don't really follow, but Charlie tells him to have fun and call if he needs to. I wipe my mouth on a napkin and insist on helping Charlie with the dishes, and he relents when he realizes that I'm not going to be swayed.

31

"So…you're a twenty-four-seven Daddy, then?" I ask when we're back in the living room.

I feel braver now. Josh talked all through dinner about his experiences as a Little, allowing me to ask questions —even ones I thought were silly— and the whole conversation made me feel normal. Or, at least, like maybe I'm in a place where I'm safe to indulge in my weird fantasies. I decide to latch on to this newfound confidence and freedom to talk about it while I can. Before my insecurities get the better of me again. Temptation simmers inside me when it comes to this man, so keeping conversation going seems like the safer option here. I mean, we only just met, and I know next to nothing about him.

Charlie shrugs. "Yeah… I guess? It's not something I can switch on and off. I mean, I don't expect to be in a relationship with someone who's Little for every waking moment. In fact, I don't want that at all. But even during adult time, I like to look after my partners, I guess."

My lips tug upward because, yeah, I can definitely see that in him. Still, I can't help but wonder whether my presence is going to throw a wrench in the works. "Will my being here interrupt something?"

"Interrupt something?" he asks, frowning. I resist the urge to smooth my thumb over the crease between his dark eyebrows.

I look at my lap, twiddling my fingers. "Like a preexisting relationship?" The words come out quiet and cautious, and I feel a pang of jealousy at the very thought. Which is ridiculous, because Charlie might have taken care of me today, but he's not mine to be jealous over.

He's silent for a minute. "Baby," he says, and once again he's tilting my chin up and forcing me to look at him. "There's nobody. But I'd like to explore our connection if you're up to it."

"Our..." I trail off, gesturing between the two of us. "As in..." I swallow. "You and me?"

My dick twitches at the suggestion. That simmering temptation threatens to boil over.

He cups my cheek and my heart thumps wildly. "Yes." His expression is almost painfully tender. "You and me."

"Y-you don't even know me," I protest, but I'm leaning into him anyway. It's magnetism.

Yes, I just got out of a relationship (one which my heart wasn't ever in, because otherwise Cooper's cheating would have actually hurt) and I've just met this man...but I can't stop myself from wanting him.

Is it too soon to feel this way? *Probably.* Is acknowledging that going to prevent me from wanting him? *Nope.*

"Which is why I said I'd like to explore the connection," Charlie answers, sounding amused. "We can go slow...but I already know your interests and mine are more than compatible." He hesitates. It almost seems strange to see the uncertainty on his face. "Unless you're not interested. That won't change the offer of a room and board, okay? I just..." He shrugs. "I'm interested in you, and I'm not gonna hide that."

I force back the urge to do a little happy dance. This seems too good to be true.

"But...I'm not sure how often I'll want to be Little."

"That's okay. Like I said, I'm not looking for someone who is always Little. I want a boyfriend to take on dates and hang out with, too."

The way he says it is guarded, and I wonder why. Is it possible his last Little didn't want that? I've read that some people want to be looked after constantly, but I grew up with a controlling father, so I can't imagine not having some semblance of independence. But I'm getting ahead of myself here.

My gut twists as another realization hits me: I can't offer Charlie *anything*.

"Well… I can't exactly bring any value to this relationship. I mean, I'm homeless and jobless and it'll look like I'm using you…"

I'm pulled into his lap midway through my rant. This is rapidly becoming a position I enjoy far too much. "Sweetheart," he assures me with soothing tones, "you're not homeless. You live here now. And you're actively looking for a job: one will turn up soon. Also, I know you're not using me. If anything, I worry that you'll feel obligated…"

"But I—"

I'm silenced with a kiss to my lips.

His kiss is everything and I'm lost to it within seconds. He kisses me chastely at first, but I open for him and our tongues twist together, finding a rhythm that feels as natural as breathing.

In his mouth, I can taste the sweetness of the cola he'd had with dinner, and I melt into him. He kisses me with intent, but it's not overwhelming. Fuck the fact that we've only just met; this feels too good to stop.

There's no pressure in Charlie's kiss, but there's obvious desire. With me straddling him on the couch, I can feel his erection pressing against mine and it's so much more intense than any other kiss I've had in my life.

Part of me wonders if that's because he knows my deepest, scariest secrets —the kinks I've been ashamed of for years— and that he accepts them… Hell, he even wants to partake in them. Or maybe it's the inherent power play. He's a Daddy and I'm... Well, I want to be his little boy.

"Oh *fuck*," I curse, feeling my balls tightening. That last thought almost sent me right over the edge. I haven't come in my pants since my early teens.

Charlie groans into my mouth. The sound is insanely hot.

Deepening the kiss, I take my pleasure from his mouth and continue to grind against him.

This should feel weird.

I hardly know this guy, and I only broke up with Cooper a few days ago —not that we'd had sex recently, come to think of it— but the blood flow to my brain isn't working so well right now. Besides, Charlie is letting me set the pace here, and I get the feeling that he'd stop the moment I asked him to.

I have no intention of doing that. People have sex with others they've just met all the time, right? Isn't that what one-night stands are? Just because we didn't meet in a club or on a hookup app doesn't mean we're not both looking for the same thing... not that I want this to be a one-night hookup, mind you. I don't think Charlie does either. Anyway, even if that is the case, the only people who can judge us in this moment are ourselves, and I get the feeling Charlie wants this as much as I do.

If he doesn't think it's weird, neither do I.

"Baby..." He breathes the word against my lips, and the gravel in his voice almost does me in. He sounds as needy as I feel. It's empowering.

My breath quickens as I rut against his answering hardness, and I know I'm going to go over the edge. I don't want to come in my pants, but I don't want to stop, either. I buck my hips and hear myself fucking *mewl*, "I... I'm gonna..."

"It's okay." Charlie's big, rough hand is at my fly. He's popping the button and lowering the zipper, and the relief once he springs my dick from the constrictive material is immediate. "I've got you."

Those beautiful, reassuring words are heaven to my ears.

I open my mouth to say something, but the words leave me because that same hand is stroking me —skin on skin, my precum easing the way— and it takes all of three pumps of his fist before I'm shooting over his hand and his shirt, crying out my release as I come.

I feel boneless as he tucks me back into my underwear but leaves my jeans undone. He wipes his hand on his already filthy shirt, and I shake off the post-orgasmic haze and reach for his cock.

"Not tonight," he says, carefully holding my wrist, and I frown. He's hard as steel in his pants. I don't understand.

"Why not?"

Charlie leans forward and presses a soft kiss to the tip of my nose. "Tonight was about you."

If I had needed any further proof that he was genuine about not pressuring me, this would do it.

Chapter Six – Charlie

I'm moving too fast. I know I am. This poor boy has been through hell this week, he's still hesitant about indulging his Little side, and here am I just taking advantage of his vulnerability. Someone needs to take my Daddy card away because the shit that I just pulled? Not cool. Not in the least. I really don't want Ash thinking that I'm only offering him the room because I expect things from him.

"Come on," I tell him, swatting his firm, pert ass to scoot him off my lap. "How about we head upstairs, do some coloring then watch a movie, hmm?"

"Coloring?" he questions.

I shrug. "Part of the lifestyle is routine. I know you're not in your Little headspace right now, but...it might help to start up a routine to give yourself some Little time every night?"

Over dinner, he'd said that he tried to give himself Little time whenever he knew he'd have a few hours alone, and that it helped him manage his stress levels. When that time became harder to come by, he felt his ability to control his emotions and his Little headspace slipping. If Little space is his coping mechanism, it makes sense that it's going to be where his brain goes when he's overwhelmed.

"Of course," I add as he stares at me with blatant skepticism, "you're free to be Little here whenever you need. Some people flow in and out of their Little headspaces in a more fluid state." I imagine this is how Ash will be as he gets more comfortable in his skin. Given my own desires, I hope he'll choose to share that lifestyle with me. I can't picture him being Little more often than not, but I can see us falling into a routine that works with my erratic work hours.

Maybe I'm projecting, but it almost feels like I've manifested the unicorn Little of my dreams.

But I'm getting ahead of myself again.

"Right." He blinks as we stand at the bottom of the stairs, giving a little shake of his head. "It's going to take a while to get used to all this, I guess. Having my urges normalized, I mean."

"They *are* normal," I insist. I'm going to repeat this mantra until it sinks in. "Sexuality is a spectrum. BDSM and kink is a spectrum within the spectrum. None of it is shameful."

His shoulders lift and droop in a helpless shrug.

"Would it help you to meet others like you? Like us?" I don't know why I'm doing this, why I'm pushing so hard when it's only his first day in my home, but I'm desperate for him to understand that he's got nothing to be embarrassed about. "Because I can take you to The Grove. It's a BDSM club, and they have a huge, dedicated space for age play. Josh was heading there tonight."

Those hazel eyes of his are round, and his mouth has formed an O of surprise. "Wow. Are there that many of us in the city?"

I nod. "Yes." And because I'm an asshole, I repeat slowly,

"Because. It's. Normal."

He surprises me by laughing. It's a gorgeous laugh. Carefree and contagious. Another glimpse into the beautiful little boy I know he'll be. "Okay." The smile he offers me is warm. "It's normal to have kinks. I get it. But, Charlie, I don't want to go to a club tonight. Maybe another time? I just…" He turns bashful. "I'd like to do what you said and…y'know…explore this thing between us for now."

How can I deny him that when I want the exact same thing? I hold his cheeks in my hands and press my lips to his in a sweet kiss that I hope imparts everything I can't put into words. "I'd like that, too."

His grin turns cheeky. "So…do I have to call you Daddy?"

My dick, which had managed to calm down from not being allowed to come earlier, swells back up almost instantly. Swallowing roughly, I shake my head. "That's a title I have to earn, baby," I inform him, "and only when you're comfortable with using it. This whole thing" —I gesture wildly— "is all about comfort and consent and, ultimately, trust. We need to talk about rules and expectations and limits…"

We'd touched on some of it over dinner. Josh's perspective had been a godsend. But if Ash and I are going to give this whole thing a shot, we need to sit down and make sure we're both on the same page. No more impromptu hand jobs or making out, until we know where we stand.

"Maybe," I say slowly, my hand finding its place on the small of his back as I guide him up the stairs, "instead of coloring, tonight we can go over some of the information online about the lifestyle? Together? And we can start talking about those things. If that's what you want."

Ash's eyes soften and his expression is filled with gratitude.

Even if I'm afraid I'm pushing him too fast and too soon, that look settles my concerns. So does his reply. "That sounds good."

So it's what we do. I change into a new T-shirt and boxers, and we settle in on the couch upstairs with our laptops balanced on our respective thighs. I let him Google and explore at his own pace, and he asks questions as he goes.

He cocks his head at me at one point, flicking his laptop screen for emphasis. "So…safe words are a thing even with regression stuff?"

"Hell yeah," I acknowledge. "Consent is the first rule of any kink play, and it has to be explicit. Even though we're not doing anything physically taxing for the most part, there's emotional and mental comfort to consider."

"Do—" He clears his throat. "Do you have a safe word?"

"I like the traffic light system." *The darling of the BDSM world.*

Those gorgeous eyes light up with excitement. "Oh, that's clever! Can I use that?"

I can't stop myself from leaning over and kissing him gently. "Of course."

He beams and then turns back to his laptop. While he's researching, I'm shopping. I'm buying him new clothes —Big and Little both— and toiletries and toys. I've ordered extra diapers and wipes and bottles, because his curiosity is rapidly turning to enthusiasm, and I want to be prepared for him. Additional groceries follow, because even if he's not officially my boy, he's living here now, and I'm going to care for and provide for him.

"So…the diaper thing," he queries softly, not long after I've placed the last of my orders.

I turn to him, trying to keep my expression neutral. It's not a surprise that he's gone there. It's one of the bigger concerns for most people new to exploring age regression. "Yeah?"

He squirms in his seat. "Is it... I mean, do people actually..."

"Wet them?"

Just the words send another delicious flush of embarrassment over Ash's skin, and I have the urge to cuddle him and never let him go. He's such a sweet boy.

He coughs. "Uh...yeah. That."

"They do, yeah." I say it as though it's not a big deal, because for me, it's not. "But that's not an immediate thing, or even expected. Some people are content to wear them purely for aesthetics or the feel of it. Others start that way and work their way up to being comfortable enough to lose themselves entirely in their Little headspace."

"*Entirely?*" he asks, then scrunches his nose. "Oh, no, sorry, *eww*. Poop is a hard limit." He gags exaggeratedly.

I can't help my burst of laughter at his horrified expression. "That's fair, baby. Totally fair." But then I can't help teasing a little, cocking an eyebrow at him. "But wetting's okay?"

"Charlie!" The blush which had faded comes back with a vengeance.

Still, he doesn't say no. I didn't expect him to. He's already admitted that he's curious about it, and my guess is he might one day genuinely enjoy the freedom that comes with letting go that way...once he trusts himself and his Daddy wholeheartedly. I smother a pang of yearning to be that Daddy. To earn that much trust from this skittish man.

Too fast, Charlie.

I blame my mother for how quickly my investment in this potential relationship has bloomed. She's notorious for her hyperactivity, too.

When Ash yawns, I glance at my watch and decide it's probably past the bedtime I would usually set for a little boy. But we've covered a lot of ground over the past couple of hours and have gotten to know each other better. After he shyly agreed that he's just as interested in an "us" as I am, we moved onto negotiations.

We've decided on some basic rules, honesty with each other being the most significant of them. He's agreed to watch his language and follow my instructions when he's Little, and we'll treat each other as equals and partners the whole way.

We went over the concept of consequences for breaking the rules, and I was clear that, in my world, spanking is a "funishment" and part of game play only. Actual consequences might range anywhere from being stood in a corner to writing lines to being grounded. He agreed with it all.

I send him off to use the bathroom and brush his teeth, and when he comes back out of the bathroom and into his bedroom, he blinks at the new pajamas I hold out to him, complete with a brand-new pair of training pants.

"Uh…" he says, looking from the clothing to me and back again.

"How long have you been cycling through the same pair of jeans with different shirts?" I ask delicately. "I'd like to throw them in the wash."

"Okay," he acknowledges after another moment's thought. Then he swallows. "Will you, um, help me get dressed?"

He's Big right now, but the step toward the relationship I so badly want to cultivate with him squeezes my heart. I can see his own longing reflected in his hazel eyes, and that convinces me that he's not just doing this because he knows I want it. He wants it, too. I'm proud of him for voicing the request. "I would love that, baby."

In his room, I help pull his plain gray T-shirt over his head, then push his jeans and underwear over his hips and down his legs. I learn that his blush travels down his neck and over his chest, and I want to kiss every spot it touches, but I don't push my luck. This is only day one. We have time.

We have forever, says a traitorously hopeful voice at the back of my head.

I ignore that voice in preference of pulling the training pants up his long legs, paying no attention to his semihard cock. I've already pushed those boundaries further than I'm comfortable with for one night. Ash scrunches his nose adorably and wriggles.

"They're tight," he complains lightly, glancing down at the spaceship print over his bulge. Then a small smile tugs at his lips. "But...I think I like them."

I'm sure my answering grin makes me look goofy as fuck, but I couldn't care less. "It makes me happy to hear that." I'm making an effort to talk to him like I would if he was Little. The routine is important for both of us and will make the transition easier for him.

I tap his left calf muscle, encouraging him to lift the leg to get his new pj's on next. These are loose cotton pants covered in paw prints. The matching shirt has a puppy on it. He steadies himself on my shoulders as I help him step into them.

When he's fully dressed, he's adorable and I tell him so.

"Thank you." He bites the corner of his lip, and my cock surges back to life again.

"We, uh, we haven't discussed sleeping arrangements," I tell him, adding, "but there's no expectation for you to sleep in my bed. Not now...and not ever if you're not comfortable with it."

"I mean, you've already jerked me off today," he teases, and the reminder of my lapse in control does nothing to ease my erection. "But…maybe for tonight, can I stay in here? Just to get my thoughts together?"

I never want him to feel uncomfortable or coerced in any way. This all has to be his choice. "Of course, sweetheart. But I'm going to leave my door open a crack, and if you need me at all during the night, call out or come get me, okay?"

Ash's expression turns soft and a little grateful. "I'd like that. Thanks, Charlie."

This beautiful boy is going to be the death of me.

Chapter Seven – Asher

I wasn't lying when I told Charlie that I liked his very Daddy-esque suggestion of keeping his door open. When I'm anxious, I'm prone to nightmares, so it's soothing to know that there's someone there just in case. *A Daddy*, my brain sing-songs helpfully.

I'm trying to ignore just how easily I'm accepting this entire change of circumstances. What are the chances that the perfect man for me is (a) single and (b) willing to move me into his home without ever having met me before? But there's absolutely no pressure coming from him to do anything that I'm not comfortable with, and he seems to genuinely want to look after me. *Me*. It's mind-boggling. Nobody has ever cared like this before. Like, *ever*.

That said, I've read enough about the Daddy mindset that I know it's not all that strange. He probably sees a Boy struggling and, because he's obviously a good man (the cop thing gives that away, not to mention how kind and caring he has been), he's driven to help. Besides that, there's a mutual attraction between us —if the impromptu hand job earlier is any indication— which doesn't hurt.

For the first time in ages, I allow myself to feel a flicker of hope that maybe I will have a chance to explore all the interests I thought I'd have to keep secret forever. This both thrills and terrifies me.

Charlie asks me my traffic light color when he goes to sit on the bed beside me. He's selected a kid's book from the shelf under the window and, even though it's late, he wants to read me to sleep.

"Green," I tell him without hesitation, ignoring the butterflies in my belly when he smiles widely.

It should feel strange to snuggle up next to this man I've known for all of a few hours, but there's something *right* about it. Maybe it's just the relief of having a roof over my head, of having a full tummy and no fear of being caught breaking rules. Whatever it is, there is nothing daunting about being tucked against his solid chest with one of those muscular arms wrapped around my shoulders, holding me in place. His large palm is smoothly stroking my side in a rhythmic up-and-down motion, and he's reading *The Poky Little Puppy* in a perfect Daddy voice, all low and lulling. I drift off into dreamland far sooner than I want to.

However, I wake up in the middle of the night with my heart pounding and a small cry of terror on my lips. The nightmare is already fading, but the fear has well and truly set in. It takes me a minute to get my bearings. There's a strip of light filtering in through the half-open doorway, and as my brain engages, I remember the day's events all over again.

I'm not quite Big, but I'm not Little either. I'm hovering in this strange mental space where I *want* to crawl out of bed and take Charlie up on his offer, but the adult in me thinks it'll be too much of an imposition. I don't need him to regret taking me in like the pathetic street urchin I've become. Clutching at my blankie, I fiddle with the fraying corner while I mull over my options and try to talk myself down from the nightmare-induced panic.

"Ash?" Charlie's voice is gravelly with sleep, and the strip of light from the living area widens as he opens my door fully. "Can I come in?"

I open my mouth to tell him I'll be fine, but the word "Please" tumbles out instead. I sound meek and vulnerable even to my own ears.

He steps inside the room, backlit from the living room light, and my breath catches. He's wearing the soft T-shirt from earlier over a pair of low-slung flannel pajama pants. His more-on-top hairstyle is all mussed from sleep, the longer strands sticking up at odd angles. He radiates raw masculinity beneath the sweet softness of his concerned-Daddy expression. My stomach does somersaults as he steps closer.

"Bad dream?" His voice is schooled into what I'm coming to recognize as his usual low, soothing tone. It makes me want to leap from the bed and throw myself into his arms.

Picking at the fraying edges of my blankie, I nod.

"Scoot over," he urges softly, and I comply without a second thought.

A voice at the back of my head tells me I'm already getting too attached, that it's dangerous to rely on him for comfort so readily, but I do my best to ignore it as Charlie climbs onto the bed beside me. He extends his arm and I cuddle up beside him without hesitation, not ignorant of the way he sighs happily.

Something about that sound silences my doubts. He genuinely wants this, too. If we both want the same things, why should I fight it?

With his arm wrapped around me again, Charlie uses that hand to card through my hair and I lean into the touch, savoring it. "Wanna talk about it?" he asks gently.

"I can't remember the dream," I explain, my eyes already getting heavy again under his gentle ministrations. "I don't usually. Just the feeling."

His hand keeps moving, his large, thick fingers massaging my scalp. "Do you have nightmares a lot?"

"Mm-hmm," I answer. "It's worse when I'm stressed." The last few nights have been full of interrupted sleep. It's probably part of why I finally broke when I was faced with the cops. With Josh.

Charlie makes a sympathetic sound, but it doesn't feel like he's pitying me. I'm glad. I hate pity. "I'm here now," he murmurs, and those words help the lingering fear recede further. "I'm here, and you're safe."

Warmth spreads through my chest and I blink back tears of relief. As embarrassing as breaking down in front of Josh was, I'm starting to think that maybe it wasn't so bad that it happened after all. Especially not if this thing with Charlie works out.

* * *

A week later, I've officially settled into Charlie's place. He had those first couple of days off, which helped us get used to living together, and then he went back to work. At first it was weird being treated like a child whenever he got home from work, but now I look forward to it. Hell, after the first few days, I've started to need it.

Charlie was right about routine helping. And now, after a week, slipping into my Little headspace in the evenings is starting to feel natural. I drift into my own little world where the stresses of adult life can't touch me. I color or watch cartoons or play with toys, and I'm in a happy little bubble where I feel safe and cared for. The feeling is addictive, and I can understand why this becomes a twenty-four-seven lifestyle for people. To be honest, even though I can't see it being an all-the-time thing, I can see myself easily slipping in and out of my Little headspace without too much drama.

And that scares me a bit, because there's still a tiny voice at the back of my mind that says it's abnormal.

However, the more time I spend being Little, especially with Charlie's encouragement, the less that voice bothers me.

I'm genuinely happier than I can ever recall being. Even when I'm Big, I'm enjoying life. I've been applying for jobs and keeping the house clean and tidy while Charlie's at work.

I still pause to pinch myself every so often, because Charlie is everything I've ever hoped for in a partner. Despite there being almost a decade between us, we're on similar wavelengths. We share the same taste in movies, argue playfully over music, and even read similar books. Conversation is consistently effortless, which surprises me because it feels like I've known him for years.

Additionally, the chemistry between us, regardless of whether I'm Big or Little, is hot as fuck. We still haven't gone beyond hand jobs (he's determined not to rush our relationship, especially while I'm still learning how to be myself in all headspaces), but his cuddles and kisses are the stuff of dreams.

And his brother is a hoot.

Most evenings, Josh drops by for dinner and lets me ask him my newest round of questions about being Little. He's become my best friend next to Charlie, and I honestly can't imagine not having either of them in my life, even though a week ago they'd been complete strangers to me.

"Whatcha thinkin' about?" Josh prods from beside me.

We're both sitting on our stools at the kitchen island, each of us coloring in while Da— *Charlie* makes dinner. Tonight, Josh is more playful than usual, and I'm starting to realize through the haze of my own Little space that he's as Little as I've ever seen him.

I tear up a bit because this is my first ever playdate with another Little.

"Chaaaaaarlie," Josh calls, sounding horrified, "Ash is *crying.*"

Da— *Charlie's* in front of me in a second, all warm blue eyes and concern. His big hand is rubbing circles on my back, and it feels so right and *so* satisfying: like a final puzzle piece clicking into place. "Baby, what's wrong?"

I beam back at him, hoping that he understands that these are happy tears. "Josh is Little," I explain, finding it hard to express myself in this headspace. "He's my friend and he's Little like me."

"*Oh.*" A smile spreads across Charlie's face, and I clap my hands because, yeah, he gets it. Plus, I get a thrill from making him happy. "Yeah, he's Little today." He ruffles my hair. "You like having a friend to play with, huh?"

I nod excitedly. "Yup! My first playdate."

His expression turns all mushy, and words I'm definitely not prepared to say dance on the tip of my tongue. It's only been a week, but I'm pretty sure I am falling hard for this man. This flawless man, with his sexy-as-sin body, and the uniform that plays right into a whole different set of kinks for me, and his perfect *Daddy-ness*. How can I feel so much, so quickly?

The blogs I've read all say that BDSM relationships tend to speed ahead more quickly than traditional ones, but this feels like a bullet train. Charlie has given me everything I've ever dreamed of and then some, and it's only been a week. What more is there to come? Has everything peaked? Will things go downhill from here?

With how good this has been, I can't help but feel like I need to steel myself for the inevitable crash.

But while I'm in my Little space, those worries don't trouble me as much. All I know is I'm happy and carefree, and I have a Little friend and an *awesome* Daddy.

An awesome Daddy who is staring at me with wide, shining eyes.

My confusion at Charlie's stunned expression must show because Josh giggles and nudges me again. "You called him Daddy and broke him."

Oh. Oops.

I aim for my most cherubic smile. "Sorry, Daddy." *Damn it.* "I mean, Charlie."

Charlie laughs a watery laugh and wraps me in one of his soul-warming hugs. "I'm happy to be your Daddy, little lamb."

And oh. *Oh.* Little lamb. That's new. That's new and I love it. But I'm too Little to explain just how much.

"*Baa*," I blurt at him instead.

Josh dissolves into a new peal of giggles and I throw my orange crayon at him.

"Chaaaarlie!" Josh complains.

It's my turn to giggle.

51

Daddy tells us both to behave and we settle back into coloring, but I'm too busy floating on air to focus on what I'm doing.

* * *

"So," I say later that night, after Josh has left and I've come out of my Little headspace. We're lying side by side in Charlie's bed, even though I've been sleeping in my own. I haven't felt ready to move into his bed, but now I can't imagine going back to mine. There was a fundamental shift in our dynamic today, and we need to talk about it. "Little lamb, huh?"

Charlie grins and runs his hand through my curls. "It seemed like a suitable nickname."

He's been on cloud nine all night. I have my guesses as to why. Still, I can't help sounding shy and insecure when I ask, "And...you're okay that I called you...*y'know?*"

He arches an eyebrow. "Do I know?"

"*Daddy.*" I sigh, feeling the blush on my cheeks. I think I've blushed more in the last week than in my entire lifetime combined. *Damn pale skin.* "You're okay that I called you Daddy?"

I squeal as Charlie pulls me snug against him and rolls over me, grinding his obvious arousal against mine. "I've been hard since you said it," he confesses, then kisses me until I'm writhing and breathless.

"Does that mean you'll finally fuck me" —I smirk— "*Daddy?*"

I know I've hit my mark when his cock twitches against me, concealed as it is by the layers that separate us. I make a note to use this newfound information whenever and wherever I can.

"Language, little lamb," Charlie teases back. But the rule only applies when I'm Little, and I'm definitely not feeling Little right now, though we have fooled around during my Little time, too.

"Baa-*fucking*-aaa," I shoot back. He laughs and the sound goes straight to my cock. I arch my hips up against him. "But seriously, I'm dying here."

"We can't have that," he agrees before kissing me again. He spears his tongue into my mouth in a deliciously filthy kiss that feels like an imitation of what he'd like his dick to do to my ass. And I'm totally on board with that.

"Lube," I beg as he pulls back and pushes up my shirt. It's got *Looney Tunes* characters on it. He'd found it at Target in the men's section, and I love it. But right now, it's gotta go. His tongue and teeth tease my nipple and I cry out. "*Fuck*. Lube. Fingers. My ass. Now." My breathing hitches when he moves to the other nipple. "*Please, Daddy.*"

Ah, the magic words. They get him moving, leaning further over me to dig through his bedside table for lube and a condom. I use the advantage of this position to unbutton his jeans and pull the zipper down. His cock pushes the material of his boxer briefs out toward me, and I palm him through the cotton, teasing over the damp spot where he's dripping precum.

"Uh-uh," he says playfully, moving out of my reach now that he's got the supplies we need in hand. "Patience."

I want to complain, but I arch my hips up from the mattress as he makes short work of pulling down my pj's and the training pants he dressed me in earlier. I pull my shirt off and throw it in the same direction that he just tossed my pants. He sits back, resting his ass on his heels as he sweeps his heated gaze over my naked body.

Obviously he's seen me naked before, but this time feels

different. There's no undercurrent of sweetness or of the cute, playful relationship between Daddy and his boy. This is all heat and longing. I take my hand to my cock and stroke it to tease him.

He groans and bats my hand away, replacing it with his. "This is mine, baby. You don't get to touch it unless I say so."

Fuck if that doesn't make me go hot all over. And with the way my dick jumps and leaks in his loose hold, there's no hiding how much I enjoy it.

"You'd better get fucking naked soon," I growl up at him, just before our mouths connect for another dirty, delicious kiss.

When he pulls away again, he smirks, still lazily stroking my cock. "Or what, Ash?"

"Or…" I try to think of a punishment I could throw his way, but his hand's far too distracting, and I'm not the dominant one in our relationship. I don't have any idea what sort of ultimatum I could give him. At least, not while I'm Big. If I were Little, I'd probably come up with something ridiculous that would have him laughing indulgently. "Or…*ugh.*" I drop my head back onto the mattress with a chuckle that morphs into a needy whine. "I don't know. Just strip already." Propping myself on my elbows, I look back up at him and bat my lashes. "Please, Daddy? I've always wanted to watch a cop-themed striptease."

Charlie laughs and shakes his head, gesturing with his free hand to the soft cotton T-shirt and the tented boxer briefs he's wearing beneath his open jeans. "Does this look like a uniform to you?"

"I have a *very* vivid imagination."

He grins but releases my erection and shuffles backward off the bed. Standing in front of me, he lifts the hem of his T-shirt and then whips the whole item over his head in a smooth move that has me questioning whether or not he actually has practice as a stripper. But then my gaze is drawn to his muscular chest, with its smattering of dark chest hair, and across to those insane biceps of his, then down the defined abs that put my lightly toned stomach to shame. He's all hard ridges, where I have a little softness to my belly. His opened jeans hang loose on his hips, and the prominent V shape of his form dips directly into the waistband of his boxer briefs like an arrow directing me to the promised land.

"Fuck me," I mutter, because this is the first time I've seen him shirtless. I've felt those abs beneath my fingers. I've even lifted his shirts before to lick at his skin. But putting the whole picture together is breathtaking. "You're the hottest man ever." My cock drips in agreement.

He preens for a moment, then hooks his fingers in the waistband of his underwear and pushes them and his jeans to the ground. His cock is glorious, as it has been the last couple of times I've glimpsed it. It's thick but not insanely long, veiny, and purpled at the head. A bead of pearly precum gathers at the tip as I eye it, and I lick my lips.

Charlie groans. "Baby, that's cruel."

"What's cruel is you still standing there instead of getting back over here and fucking me with that monster of yours."

I've jerked him off a couple of times now, but I haven't really gotten to take him in, and I can't stop looking. Can't stop imagining what he tastes like. What he's going to feel like inside me. He's definitely bigger than either of the two men I've been with before, and that's slightly daunting.

"Hey." Charlie crawls back over the bed until we're face-to-face again. Concern has his eyebrows pulling together.

"Where'd you go just now?"

I want to laugh it off, but our first rule is honesty, so I reach for his cock and spread some of his precum over his length, slowly stroking him as I confess, "I've only been with two other guys..." I'm only twenty-two and not an extrovert, so I'm sure this doesn't come as a huge shock to him. He nods. "And you're, uh, bigger than either of them was."

Instead of grinning or laughing or acting like he's won some sort of competition, Charlie gives me a soft smile full of understanding. He scooches in closer, gently rocking his hips toward mine until our cocks brush against each other and *fuck*, that feels good. "If you're not comfortable, baby, we can stop any time, okay? We can just do this instead." He has the lube in his hand and pops the cap with his thumb, drizzling a little of the liquid down between us, and I catch it with my palm and spread it over our connecting erections.

Holy fuck.

How the hell does this feel so good?

I give in to the sensations for a moment, rocking up to meet him, squeezing both our shafts together, groaning as electricity seems to zap through my veins. Then I come back to the conversation. "I want..." I say, as though that's actually going to explain anything. But the pleasure is making it difficult for the words to come out. I try again. "I want you to fuck me. I really, really do." I swallow. "Can we just...take it slow?"

There's a part of me that wants to say 'screw that' and go fast, demanding that he take me hard and rough so I can feel him for days; but I'm smart enough to know that, at least for our first time, I'd regret it.

"Of course, baby." I get the feeling that he had no intention of doing otherwise anyway.

Charlie brings our mouths together in a sweet, sensual kiss, and before long I'm spreading my legs and guiding his fingers to my hole. Then there's lube, and he's teasing the rim slowly, pushing the pad of his finger in and out maddeningly, and I break the kiss both to praise and to complain, "Oh my God, Charlie…"

He turns prep, which has only ever been a perfunctory, mandatory thing in my previous relationships, into exquisite foreplay. There's a fuck-ton of lube used, but soon I'm writhing on three thick digits. I'm arching off the bed as he hooks his fingers and brushes my prostate again and again until I'm certain I'm going to come without even touching my cock. I'm babbling and begging, and I swear that he's edging me, until the crinkle of the foil condom wrapper has me sighing in bliss because —*fucking finally*— my Daddy is going to fuck me into the mattress.

He takes his time, rocking into me slowly, his lubed hand working my cock to distract me from the initial discomfort and burn of the intrusion. And yeah, he's bigger than I've had before, but after he bottoms out and I breathe for a moment, I love the full feeling of him inside me.

"Move," I say. I urge him by rocking my hips up, even though he's got me pretty much pinned to the mattress; he's supporting his weight now on his forearms, which are on either side of my head. I begged for this position, needing to see his face, to feel his warmth spread over me, and it's everything I hoped it would be.

"You're so perfect around me, baby," Charlie's voice is raspy and strained, "and it's been a while for me. I'm not gonna last."

That makes me feel even better. I'm the reason he's on the razor's edge. I'm the reason he's got that almost-pained, blissed-out look on his face. *Me*. It's a heady feeling.

"Me too," I admit as he starts the slow drag back out and then thrusts back in. With a swivel of his hips *just so*, he grazes my prostate again. "Fuck, *yes*. Right there."

He repeats the movement. My cock, pinned between our bodies, dribbles precum and we're pressed so close together that it's smearing between us. There's a slick-enough slide and friction there that I don't think either of us needs to wriggle a hand in to stroke it.

Again and again, Charlie repeats the movement that's making me whimper and groan, and I can feel a delicious pressure building inside me. The wave of my orgasm is cresting. I'm too fucking close but I don't want to stop it.

"You feel so good," Charlie insists, and he does the swivel–thrust thing again.

My balls tighten. White light sparks behind my eyes. The coil of tension inside me is perilously close to snapping.

"I… Charlie, *Daddy*, I… I'm…" His hips go again and I'm flying. "*Coming!*" I cry, pushed over the edge with that last thrust. Neither of us has actually touched my cock, and yet I'm spurting ropes of cum between us, and with his body pressed against mine and his movements picking up, it's spreading everywhere. It's filthy and amazing and my dick makes an effort to jerk again because this entire experience has been so intensely hot.

"Fuck." Charlie draws the word out as he follows me over the edge, his hips stilling and his cock jerking as he releases into the condom, still deep inside me.

I wince as he carefully pulls out. He kisses my stomach, heedless of the mess there, before he backs off the bed and goes to dispose of the trash. He returns with a couple of warm, damp cloths and cleans me up before he does himself.

I fall asleep snuggled up next to him, naked and sated.

Chapter Eight – Charlie

I've created a monster. In the two weeks since we first had sex, Ash has jumped me at every opportunity. I'm thirty-one and I don't consider myself old by any means, but I'd completely forgotten what the libido of a twenty-two-year-old was like. And let's not get started on his refractory period. That boy can come five times in a two-hour period. *Five.* That has to be a superpower. I consider myself lucky when I can get it up a second time within an hour.

Josh thinks it's hilarious. I mean, of course he would; he's twenty-three. He's got the same boundless energy as my boyfriend.

Boyfriend.

The word still makes me all warm and fuzzy inside. But not as much as "Daddy" does. It doesn't get old, hearing my little lamb call me by the title. Whether it's during sex or spoken in his higher-pitched, almost innocent Little Ash voice, it's music to my ears.

In the three weeks we've been together, I've watched him

come out of his shell. He's no longer the anxious, confused mess he had been when I first set eyes on him. He's still got reservations about fully letting go and sinking deep into his Little headspace, but he goes further and further every time, and with each day we learn something new about Little Ash.

Josh has been beyond helpful with that process. When Ash admitted that having playdates made it easier to dip into his Little space, Josh was more than happy to join him. Most evenings, they color, play with blocks, or —as they did a couple of nights ago— create stories together using Ash's ever-growing pile of stuffed toys as a cast of characters in their imaginative play.

As much as I've enjoyed watching Ash begin to discover his Little side, it's been a revelation watching my brother indulge his own. He might argue that he's just a scene player, but I'm not so sure that's the case. I have my suspicions about his actual desires, but I'm not going to push him. If he wants to talk about it, he knows where to find me.

When I walk through the front door tonight, thankfully at a reasonable hour, I'm not surprised that Ash greets me at the front door. However, I am surprised that he's Big. Our usual routine sees him indulging in Little time before dinner and Big time before bed. After sex, he alternates depending on his mood.

"I got a job!" he cheers, and I beam at him because I know it's been eating away at him.

He deferred his studies, deciding that with only a semester left to go, it would be silly not to finish them one day. But he's continued to stress about not contributing to bills, even though it's not something I care about.

I wrap him in my arms as he throws himself at me, and I spin us around while he laughs. "Baby, that's fantastic news!" I'm unable to stop myself from cupping his jaw and kissing those ridiculously plump lips of his. "Which job?"

As we head into the dining room, he holds my hand and pushes me down into one of the chairs at the table, facing it sideways away from the table itself. Straddling my lap and looping his arms behind my neck, he says, "Administrative assistant at a law firm downtown."

"Oh" —I smirk— "*fancy*. Does that mean I get to see you in a suit?"

He nods, but the smile slips. "I don't have a suit. Or any corporate clothing."

"We can fix that," I assure him, but I know this is going to lead to one of the only things we ever argue about.

When he's Little, Ash is oblivious to my buying new things for him. But when he's Big, he's guilt ridden and doesn't understand how much I enjoy providing for him. Some part of me wonders whether his awful father made him feel like a burden and a leech, but it's not a topic I'm willing to bring up. I'd much rather just spoil him and make up for any shortfalls in his old life.

"I—" he starts, but I press my index finger to his lips.

"No arguments. I'm buying you what you need."

Ash pouts and then sucks my finger into his mouth, twirling his tongue around it.

Moaning in response, I lift my hips up, my hardening cock finding his. "You're a pest," I accuse, but it's without heat. "I have to make dinner."

"Or," he drags the word out, slipping off my lap and to his knees in front of me, "I could help you with *this* now." He palms my obvious erection.

We've both been tested recently, so after a talk we decided to ditch condoms, which means blow jobs are infinitely more enjoyable for both of us. "God, baby." I run my hand through his soft curls, musing absently that he's probably due a haircut. "You're going to be the death of me."

That's all the permission he needs. His nimble fingers undo my belt and the button above my fly, then he's unzipping my pants and tugging my cock out of my underwear through what little space he's created. He kisses the tip sweetly before licking the head as though it's a lollipop. He's teasing me and I love every second of it.

But he's got very little patience and it's not long before he's taking as much of my cock into his mouth as he can, wrapping his hand around the base because my cock doesn't quite fit without him gagging. His mouth is heaven, all warm, wet suction, and it's not going to take him long to get me off. Especially not when I hear his zipper go down, the snick of the cap of a bottle of lube, and then the wet sound of his hand shuttling up and down his own cock.

The idea that he's planned for this, to the point of having lube with him, is heady and arousing as fuck, and I tell him so.

He moans around me while he sucks and bobs his head, and the vibrations inch me closer to the edge of my orgasm. "Baby," I warn him, my voice tight and gruff, "I'm close."

He sucks harder, his hand works faster, and with a shout I lift off from the chair and come hard down his throat. He sucks and licks me clean until the hypersensitivity is too much, and I gently push his head away. I glance down just in time to watch him spurt over his hand and onto the polished timber between his spread knees.

"That's my good boy," I praise, and he grins up at me with

the most lust-drunk expression I've seen on his face, his eyes half-lidded and dopey.

He's gorgeous, I think. *He's gorgeous, and he's all mine.*

* * *

Two weeks later, it's official: Asher loves his job. Suit shopping had been fun for us both, as had the intense orgasms we'd shared after we'd gotten home, both riled up from teasing each other during the shopping trip. He looks at ease in business pants and a crisp dress shirt, almost as natural as he does in training pants and a onesie. The two sides of him couldn't be more different, but the dichotomy captivates me.

It turns out I really do like having my cake and eating it, too.

I get to be Daddy, but I also get the partner that I've always wanted. We're equals as adults. We get to hang out, have a beer, see grown-up movies…but we also get to indulge our other needs, too. I get to play make-believe with him, or with race cars or blocks, read him books, bathe him and give him nightly snuggles…and neither of us feels like we're missing out on anything. Or, at least, that's my impression.

"So, are you ever going to introduce your boy to your friends, or will he be your little secret forever?" Josh asks me over lunch.

"He's not a secret," I snap back, feeling far more defensive than I should. I jab a carrot stick in his direction. I've been packing Asher's lunch and my own at the same time, and it's just easier to prep the same snacks for both of us. "We've only been together, like…" I tilt my head from side to side, as if I don't know that it's been exactly five weeks and three days. "…five weeks."

"Uh-huh." Josh gives me a look that says I'm not fooling

anyone. "You're head over heels for him already, big brother. Does it matter how long it's been? And also, don't you think the guys are gonna start poking their noses in if you don't touch base?"

I shrug. My friends are all fairly easygoing, and they get that my work schedule is unpredictable. We can go months at a time without catching up, and I've been staying somewhat involved in the group chat, so they know I'm alive. "They'll meet him eventually."

The guys in question —Chance, Spencer and Ted— are Daddies like me. I met Ted at The Grove years back when I was getting involved with my first Little and needed some mentoring. Spencer and Chance came along in a similar fashion when our littles at the time were close and had playdates often. All four of us have been in and out of relationships with littles in recent years, and Spence is the only one of us currently in a long-term relationship, since he has his Little, Emma.

Well, he *was* the only one. Now that I have Asher, that makes two of us, I suppose. Ash and I may only have been together for a couple of months, but I can see us being together long-term. Maybe the guys really *should* meet him soon. Damn Josh for being right. *Again.*

Josh sometimes joins our circle of friends, but he's usually more comfortable when other subs are around. I understand that all the Daddy Dom attention can be overwhelming when you're the only sub, especially when you're a brat like my brother.

I've waited too long to respond, though, and Josh's impatience wins out. "Okay, look, I might have an ulterior motive," he admits when his initial line of questioning fails to get him the result he wants.

Arching an eyebrow, I lean back in my seat. "This should be interesting."

"I met a new Little at The Grove and I think he'd be good for Chance."

Huh. Not what I'd expected. "You know I'm not into matchmaking, J."

He holds up his hands in surrender. "I know, I know. But he's new to town and he's into all that gaming stuff like Chance is…" He shrugs. "Plus he's hot. A bit older than most boys, and a lot bulkier, but Chance has never gone for the young twink type."

I find it ironic that Josh is talking about not fitting the boy stereotype. With the way he's built, nobody could call him a twink, either.

"I don't matchmake," I reiterate with a sigh. "But if he's looking to make friends who understand the lifestyle, sure. I'll organize a get-together with the guys, and you should invite him along. If nothing else, he and Ash might hit it off." My boy would probably love some additional playdates with other littles.

And that's how, a week later, I wind up hosting a potluck at my house on my next weekend off.

I've got the grill fired up in the backyard with burgers cooking, and I'm keeping a cautious eye on Asher, who keeps glancing nervously at the clock. The guys are going to start arriving in the next fifteen minutes or so, and the closer we get to that point, the more anxious Ash seems.

"Josh," I say, and I sigh when another glance in Asher's direction is met with more fidgeting and lip biting. "Watch these patties for me."

He takes over without argument, and I make my way to my boyfriend. He's Big right now but squirming and clearly nervous. "Come on, babe." I usher him inside, into the living room where his blankie is draped over the couch. He clutches at it the second we sit. "Talk to me."

"I don't want to embarrass you in front of your friends," he admits, and there's a hint of Little Ash in the way he speaks. It's been a while since I've seen him quite so anxious, and I hate that I'm responsible for it. Even though Ash and I had talked about this meeting and his potential concerns the night Josh brought the idea up, I should have known he'd panic.

"Little lamb, you won't. I promise."

His lower lip wobbles.

"If you wanna be Little for today, nothing's stopping you."

Those hazel orbs go wide with abject horror. "In front of strangers? Fuck no."

"Language," I say to correct him, and he arches an eyebrow.

"The rule is only while I'm Little, Charlie."

"You're not entirely Big right now," I reason.

Ash moves to argue and then sighs. "No, you're right. I'm… God, I don't know what I am."

"Nervous," I say, keeping my tone soft and supportive. "And that's okay. But baby…Little or Big, they're gonna love you." I've already told him that the guys are all involved in the same kink circle, and that none of them would ever judge Asher or me. "If anything, I'm gonna have to keep my eye on Ted. He might try to steal you away."

Ted's in his midforties and is probably the person I'd call my best friend, aside from Josh. He talked me through all of my concerns when I took on my first Daddy role, and he's a calming influence in my life. Almost like a big brother, something I never had growing up, what with being the eldest of four. Josh is the third born; we have a sister, Maisy, in between us, and our youngest sibling is Axel, who is in his senior year of high school. I've already told Ash all of this, too. But I haven't told Ash that, yeah, Ted and I seem to share very similar tastes.

Telling him as much now has the desired effect. He laughs and shakes his head, relaxing in his seat. "He's got zero chance of that."

"I'm glad to hear it."

We talk through his concerns a little more until he's as relaxed as I'm going to get him. And when the doorbell rings and he doesn't freeze up, I count that as a win.

Chapter Nine – Asher

Charlie's friends are actually awesome. His best friend, Ted, hasn't arrived yet, but everyone else has, and so has Josh's new friend, Matteo. He asks to just be called Matt, and everyone's doing just that.

When Josh told me that Matt's a Little like us, I thought he was kidding. If anyone could look more like a Dom, it would be Matt. But, then again, Josh doesn't exactly fit the sub mold either. And, if I'm being really honest, I'm also not exactly a twink. Of the three of us, though, I'm definitely the closest fit to the stereotype.

Then there's Emma, Spencer's Little girlfriend. She's gorgeous. Today she's Big like the rest of us, but her hair's still in long, dark pigtails and her lips are painted bright pink. She's as bubbly as the brightly colored dress she's wearing, and I'm immediately comfortable talking to her.

The two Daddies, Chance and Spencer, aren't exactly intimidating, though. Chance looks like an ordinary guy in his midthirties. He's got a bit of a dad bod, a scruffy reddish beard, and his hair is cropped really short because, according to him, it's starting to thin. Spencer is tall and lanky, with glasses and wild dark hair. But he has a friendly smile, and the way he looks at Emma makes me feel all fizzy inside because it's a lot like the way Charlie looks at me.

We're all lounging around the big outdoor dining table nursing beers —or wine coolers for Emma and me— when the doorbell rings. Charlie looks over his shoulder at me before he goes to answer it, and I smile widely at him. It means a lot to me that he's always checking in, even if only with a glance here and there.

I'm still grinning when he brings Ted through.

And then my stomach drops.

"Holy shit," I say under my breath, because *Ted* is Theodore Masters. The senior partner at the law firm I've just started working for. He might be dressed down in jeans and a dark Henley, but it's still the same man. My boss. My boss's boss, if I want to get technical. "Shit. Shit. Fuck."

"Hey." Josh is closest to me, and his hand moves to my back. It's not quite as good as Charlie's, but it's helping to stave off the anxiety attack of my boss discovering my secret life. And yeah, if I were thinking rationally, I'd realize that I've also just discovered his, but being outed as a Daddy is much less disturbing in my books. "Ash," he says softly, "breathe."

This doesn't really help because all it does is bring everyone's attention my way. Including Charlie's. How the hell could Charlie not have connected the dots that the law firm I work for is the same one where his best friend is senior partner? Or did he know and just not tell me?

"Baby." Charlie's hand has replaced Josh's and he's rubbing slow, soothing circles at my back. I can feel how red my face is, but I can't look up. Not at the people around the table. Not at Charlie. "Baby, talk to me."

I shake my head. I can't. I can't do words right now.

"I think I'm the issue," Ted's voice offers — a voice I've heard around the office and always thought of as paternal. He sounds chagrined and a little apologetic.

Beside me, Charlie sounds confused. "How?" The part of me that worried he'd kept the information from me relaxes a tiny bit.

"Asher's the firm's newest admin assistant," Ted answers easily, and I still can't look up. "And I imagine it's jarring to have the boss just saunter in on a gathering like this."

He doesn't spell it out. Doesn't have to. We all know what we are.

"Well. Fuck." I want to laugh at Charlie's assessment, but I can't. Instead, I'm still paralyzed by anxiety.

I feel ridiculous because, honestly, the situation should be comedic. But the part of me that's terrified of people finding out that I'm *abnormal* can't be reasoned with.

Charlie continues and he's close enough that I can feel him shaking his head. "I didn't know. How the hell did I miss that?"

"The firm was bought out recently. It changed names a few months back. You probably didn't recognize it." Ted's voice is getting closer, and I squeeze my eyes shut because I don't want this. I don't want to have this conversation. Not with my boss's boss. Not in front of all of Charlie's friends.

But it's happening anyway, because on my other side, where Josh was sitting, the tall, imposing figure that is Theodore Masters crouches down. I catch the movement out of the corner of my eye. "It's alright," he says in a low, gentle voice. "Why don't you head inside with your...with Charlie and take

71

a minute to process, okay?"

There are probably all sorts of meaningful glances being exchanged above my head. I'm flooded with embarrassment and hating that I can't just react to this situation like a normal person. Surely I should just be able to laugh it off and say "Ha, well that was awkward, let's never speak of this at work" and let that be the end of it. But I can't.

A couple of seats away, Emma's bright voice cuts into the tension. "Daddy, I have to go potty. Can you take me?"

I want to hug her, because it's obvious that she's trying to take the attention off me. She was Big; there was no other reason for her to ask the question. The sound of chairs scraping tells me people are moving around, and in that moment, I feel free to take advantage of the distraction. I launch from my seat and practically race into the house and up the stairs. I know that Charlie's on my heels, but I don't wait for him.

I practically fling myself into my kid's bed, even though I haven't slept in it in weeks. I try to burrow under the covers, but Charlie's slipping in beside me before I get the chance.

"I had no idea, Ash. I would have warned you if I did."

"I know," I answer. "And I know that it doesn't change anything, him knowing about me being…"

"Little?"

I think we both know I was going to say something derogatory. But I nod. "I just… I panicked and then I couldn't stop panicking and now I've humiliated myself and ruined your get-together with your friends—"

As usual, Charlie pulls me into his lap midway through my freak-out. He's rocking me gently and pressing kisses to the top of my head, and I'm struck by the thought that I'm not just falling for this man, I'm actually in love with him. What a great time to have that revelation.

Well done, Scanlon. Idiot.

"You haven't ruined a damn thing, little lamb." He's gentle and reassuring. "They all understand."

I shake my head. "You can do so much better than a broken Little who's prone to stupid panic attacks."

"Hey, stop it." The gentleness is gone from his tone. This is one hundred percent Daddy admonishment. He manhandles me in his lap, turning me and forcing my chin upward. "Look at me, Asher."

I do as he asks because I can't ignore that tone.

His blue eyes are soft and full of emotions that I'm too afraid to put a name to. "Baby, you're not broken. And panic attacks happen to everyone." When I scoff, he frowns. "Do you know how many cops have PTSD or other anxiety disorders? Or marines, or firefighters, or any other first responders or members of the armed forces?" I swallow and shake my head, and Charlie keeps talking. "Or any career, really. Anxiety isn't limited to any one kind of person, and it doesn't mean you're broken if you're struggling with it." He presses his forehead to mine. "But if you genuinely feel this way, I want to help you. I think… I think maybe you should talk to someone. A professional."

I want to argue that I don't need therapy, but when I open my mouth to do that, the words die on my tongue. With my panic receding, I consider the situation downstairs and conclude that there was no real reason to react like I did. My issues are in my head, and pushing them down or pretending they don't exist isn't going to make them go away.

"Okay," I agree quietly, much to Charlie's surprise. "I think you're right."

When he finally coaxes me back downstairs, I'm tense with embarrassment but nobody treats me any differently. I still apologize to the table for my freak-out, but everyone scrambles to shut the attempt down quickly. I eventually relax back into conversation, quietly thanking Emma for her diversion, and she shrugs and says she likes to dip into her Little headspace at random anyway. I can relate to that, and it helps me relax a bit more.

As the evening ends and people start leaving, I note that Ted's hanging around and resign myself to having to talk to him after all. I've avoided him for the afternoon, but I also know that he's my Daddy's best friend and not talking to him isn't going to help anything.

While Charlie talks to Spencer about arranging a playdate for me and Emma —who has slipped back into her Little headspace quite happily and is swinging Spencer's hand between them while sucking her thumb— Ted pulls me aside.

"I really am sorry for earlier, Ash," he says, and I blink at him.

Objectively, he's a handsome man. His brown hair is on its way to gray, and he fits the whole silver-fox vibe well, even if the 'silver' part is still developing. He's not as well built as Charlie or Josh, but he's still tall and broad shouldered, with a toned stomach and a butt that looks pretty damn good in those jeans of his. Not that I was looking, of course. His eyes are more amber than Josh's darker-brown orbs, and they're warm as he looks at me. It settles any of my remaining nerves.

"Why are you sorry? I'm the one who lost it and made a scene."

Ted shakes his head. "Without any warning, your boss wandered into a gathering where you were supposed to feel safe and relaxed. In your place, I'd have felt apprehensive as well." He reaches out and squeezes my shoulder. "But in some ways, this is a good thing. If you're ever in need of a safe space at work for any reason, come to my office. I can get you comfortable and call Charlie."

I can't help but well up with affection for him because it's such a thoughtful offer. I doubt I'll ever take him up on it, but just knowing that he'd do that for Charlie's sake tells me he's a good guy. "Thank you," I say, because there's not much else I can. "I appreciate that."

Then he hugs Charlie goodbye, and once Ted's gone, it's just the two of us left. I slip into my Little headspace a lot quicker than usual, and Daddy seems to understand.

"It's been a big day, huh, little lamb?" he asks, holding my hand as we climb the stairs.

"Yup," I agree, the stress and panic melting away the deeper I sink into my Little space.

"How does an early bath sound?"

I practically bounce on the balls of my feet. "Bath time!" I love bath time. There's something super relaxing about the combination of warm water and bubbles. Plus the splashing! Splashing makes everything better.

"Okay, bud, go potty and I'll get the water running."

I walk over to the toilet, not even blinking at the fact that Daddy's still in the bathroom, and then frown down at my jeans. Suddenly, the button and zipper seem like a lot of work. Biting my lip, I squirm.

"Ash, you okay?"

I don't even hesitate. "Help?"

In the back of my mind, I know this is another step forward for us. The toileting thing is not something either of us have discussed beyond my original questions. But after hearing Emma ask for help today, something's clicked and my curiosity's piqued. Worst case, this will feel too weird, and I won't ask again. But none of that's really at the forefront of my thoughts right now. Not with the running water going and the sudden desperate urge to pee.

"You sure?" Daddy asks, because he's obviously more cautious than I am. "Traffic light?"

"*Green.*" A little frustration bleeds into my voice. I'm wriggling now, trying to stave off an accident. "I need to go potty." The running bath water is all I can hear. "I need to go *bad.*"

His hands quickly undo the button and zipper and tug down my constrictive training pants. The respite is instantaneous, but I'm not so Little that I need him to help me aim right now. He chuckles and backs away at my sigh of relief as I evacuate my bladder.

That was too close.

A part of me feels far too curious about what might have happened if I had wet myself, but that's smothered quickly. Pushing that boundary is just a bit too far out of my comfort zone. Too close to my hard limits about humiliation, even while I'm Little. But it does kind of remind me of my curiosity about diapers...and *using* them.

After I wash my hands, Daddy helps pull my shoes and socks off, then my pants and underwear, and finally my shirt over my head. Then he guides me into the bath and laughs as I happily splash about. He's given me my favorite toy boat, and my duckie, and asks me questions about their adventures as they go plowing through the cascade of bubbles.

"Ready for me to wash you?"

The water's getting tepid, so I nod. I'm used to this now.

He dunks a washcloth under the water, squeezes some body wash onto it, and glides it over my skin. Some nights this gets me hard, but I'm too Little to be distracted by the sensations tonight. Not even when he gets me to lift up so he can wash my dick and my bottom.

We washed my hair last night, so tonight there's no need to get my hair wet. Instead, after I'm rinsed off and Daddy declares me clean, he pulls the plug and helps me out, drying me thoroughly with the waiting fluffy towel.

When we get to my bedroom, he pulls out my pj's as usual; but instead of my training pants, he grabs a diaper.

My eyes go wide. Even though I'm Little, I'm still anxious about this. But, given that I came close to peeing all over the floor barely twenty minutes ago, I can see why this is the next logical step. Hell, my own thoughts drifted that way earlier, too.

"Traffic light?" Daddy says, watching my face very closely.

"Green…and a bit yellow?"

He smiles and pats the bed. "Up." I comply, my gaze drawn to the item still in his hand. "Wanna explain the yellow?"

Licking my lips, I force my Big thoughts forward. "It's…a big step," I manage to get out. "Like…am I going to feel silly?" But my cock is twitching, giving away my interest. There's no hiding that. "I… I don't have to use it, though, right?"

"No, not at all." Charlie's staring down at me with a huge smile. "But I'm so proud of you for being brave enough to try wearing it. And if you hate it, we'll take it off and add it to the hard limits list."

Somehow, I don't think I'm going to hate it, and we both seem to recognize that. But I still nod and settle back into my Little headspace. It only takes a few moments. "Okay, Daddy."

He beams back at me, then gently taps the side of my left thigh. "Bridge." Planting my feet on the mattress, I lift my hips up and hear the crinkle of the diaper as he gets it positioned under my butt. "Okay, down."

The padded surface beneath me is…curious. It's obviously thicker than my training pants, but not entirely unpleasant. Daddy's hands smooth a barrier cream over me in slow, sensual movements that, even Little, I really enjoy. I'm powdered next, and then Daddy brings the front of the diaper up between my legs and smooths it over my semihard cock, which *really* seems to like this new kind of stimulation. His lips quirk upward, but he doesn't mention it as he brings one adhesive tab across the side and front of the diaper, and then does the same on the other. He runs his fingers along the inseams, checking the fit and making sure the leak guards are secure. Not that I'm planning on testing them.

"How does that feel?" Daddy asks me.

I wriggle a little, testing out the odd weight of it. "Strange, but…soothing? Uh, reassuring, even?" As the assessment leaves my lips, it hits me. In an instant, I know that even though I'm not comfortable using a diaper right now, one day I will be.

That thought frightens me. It makes me feel weird and wrong: no grown-ass man should consider peeing in a diaper, right? Except it's an accepted part of the age-regression lifestyle, so it's a hang-up I have to get over…and despite the lingering concerns that it's abnormal, I really, really want to get past it.

"Okay, where'd you go? Those weren't Little thoughts."

Daddy's getting way too good at reading me nowadays.

With burning cheeks, I explain my thought process, and he reassures me that these feelings are normal, that there's no rush, but that he'll be more than happy to change me it when it happens.

When. Not *if.*

I add that to my mental list of "conversations I never thought I'd have with another man" and move on.

The pj's he's selected for me are actually a footie onesie with snaps along the inseams of my legs. I'm more than aware that they're there to make it easier for changing diapers, and that thought should not make my dick even harder, but it does. When I get up to model the ensemble for Daddy, I can feel myself waddling, unused to the shape and bulk of my newest Little accessory. It feels kind of ridiculous, but the besotted expression on Daddy's face is totally worth it.

Well, that and how much I secretly enjoy it, too.

Chapter Ten – Charlie

⊱❦⊰

Ash in a diaper is easily the cutest thing I've ever seen. Ever. The fact that he wakes up hard as a rock the morning after I put the first one on him and tells me that he wants me to rub him to orgasm through the padding is hotter than it has any right being.

"You're not allowed to play with yourself when you wear one of these," I tell him, but my hand is over the hard bulge of his arousal anyway, and he's rocking up against it. "Not unless I say it's okay."

"Uh-huh," he answers, but I don't think he's actually listening to this new rule. "Daddy, it feels so good."

At least cleanup is going to be quick and easy, but I don't tell him that this is not how he should wet all his diapers. I know that's a line he's not ready to cross yet. I'm proud that he was able to voice that he's serious about trying one day, though. It's yet another big step forward for him.

"That's it, baby," I murmur, watching the rapture on his face. I give him a squeeze through the plastic and cotton, and he moans. Ash doesn't often wake up Little, or even Little adjacent, so I'm indulging the both of us right now. I'll rub one out in the shower after this. "Come for me, little lamb."

After a few more thrusts he does just that, crying out in pleasure before going limp and sated. I watch him, and a few moments later he crinkles his nose and squirms. It's adorable. "Ugh…"

"Need a change?"

He nods, and I walk him back into his room, laying out a towel before getting him to climb onto the bed. "We'll just get you into your big boy clothes after we take care of this, okay?"

"Training pants?"

"Always." Even under his suits, they've become his preference. They keep his Little urges content and remind him he has a Daddy who loves him enough to help him get dressed.

I don't make a big deal of stripping the diaper off or of wiping him down. By the time he's clean, he's Big and grinning at me. "I could get used to that being our new morning routine," he says playfully.

"Speak for yourself." I gesture at the tent in my boxers. "I need to do something about this before I can function."

Ash sits up, still naked, and scoots down the mattress until he's sitting on the edge of the bed and I'm standing between his spread legs. He grabs at my ass, pulling me closer, then mouths over the top of my erection through the cotton of my shorts. My hands card through his hair, more to steady myself than encourage him.

"How about I take care of Daddy now?"

It's not an offer I can refuse.

* * *

When we first retrieved Ash's car from the college parking structure, I'd had every intention of taking it to a mechanic for a proper evaluation. But he didn't use it for the first few weeks of living with me, and then when he got his job, it was too late. So it comes as no surprise to me when he calls me near the end of my shift one evening to complain that the thing won't start.

"It's probably just the battery," I tell him, even though I honestly know nothing about cars. "But I get off work in half an hour. Can you chill at the office until I can swing by to get you?"

"Yeah." He sighs heavily. "Stupid car. I wanted to get home early to cook you dinner. Switch things up a bit."

Awww. My boy's incredibly thoughtful.

"We can get takeout and crash on the couch," I reply. "And you can surprise me with your cooking skills another time."

From the driver's seat of our patrol car, Max makes kissy faces at me, teasing me like a good partner should. I give him the finger. Then a call comes in on the radio, and we're the closest to it. My heart sinks as I conclude that I'm not getting off work on time after all, and I have to relay the information to Ash.

"It's fine," he assures me, but there's a tension to his voice that I don't like. "I'll... I'll catch the bus home and there'll be something for you to heat up for dinner."

We say our goodbyes and I call Josh, asking him if he can go rescue my boyfriend from his broken-down piece-of-shit car. When Josh can't —because he's also stuck at work— I relent and call Ted, belatedly realizing that I should have just called him to start with.

I can hear the jangle of his keys as he agrees, and he keeps me on the line as we chat while he jogs down from the office to their allocated parking garage. "Okay," he eventually says, "I see him. I'll take him back to my place and you can pick him up on your way home, whenever that might be."

"You're a lifesaver, man," I say gratefully, then end the call. Max has an eyebrow raised, but we've just pulled up at the address we're supposed to be attending to and we need to focus on our jobs.

I'm just relieved to not have to worry about Ash.

* * *

By the time I make it to Ted's place, I'm exhausted. The call had been a domestic violence dispute that turned devastatingly ugly, and we had to take a billion witness statements, talk to paramedics, and alert child services because there was a kid involved. I'm beyond brittle by the time I ring Ted's doorbell.

When he answers the door and takes one look at me, he ushers me into his state-of-the-art kitchen and shoves a beer in my hand.

"Your boy is napping," he says, tilting his head toward his playroom. "Tuckered himself out with the train set."

I take a healthy swig from the bottle in my hand and hiss through my teeth as the liquid hits the back of my tongue. "I'm surprised he was comfortable enough to be Little around you," I say, then recall how deeply Little he was after the nearly disastrous get-together at my place. "Did he go to the bathroom before he crashed?"

"He did. And no, he didn't need my help."

It's a relief to have a friend who understands the lifestyle, and I feel a tiny bit guilty for being pleased that Ash is only comfortable enough to be that Little for me.

"Just a heads-up, though," Ted adds, and the tension is back in my shoulders. "He had a pretty shitty day at work. We've got auditors here, and they made a lot of demands on the admin staff."

All I want to do is storm into that playroom and wrap my boy in a hug. "Then his car wouldn't start, and I couldn't be there for him." Guilt eats away at me.

Ted's hand squeezes my shoulder. "None of that is your fault, and he knows it."

It still doesn't make me feel any better. "I'm his Daddy. I'm supposed to—"

"Charlie, you need to trust him as much as he trusts you. You're in a consenting adult relationship together. Remember that. Besides, Ash isn't a full-time Little, and it's pretty obvious that your job is also stressful right now."

Well. Damn. "I hate it when you're right."

"I'm always right."

I laugh, and more of the tension from today slips away. Then there are footfalls behind me and a sleepy "Charlie?"

"Hey, babe." I set down my beer and turn to face Ash. He's got a crease across his cheek from whatever he'd fallen asleep on, and his flop of curls is all mussed. Even though he's in his business pants and dress shirt, he's adorable. I open my arms, and he walks into my embrace, kissing my cheek.

"Long day?" he asks me, nuzzling into the short beard I've grown.

"Yeah. I hear yours was pretty crappy, too."

"Ugh, don't remind me." He pulls away to grin at Ted, and it makes me so happy to see them getting along. "Thanks for the rescue, by the way. And the nap. I needed both."

"I told you," Ted brushes him off, waving his own beer in

the air between us, "any time. And if tomorrow's anything like today, head into my office and steal some Little time if you need to relax and regroup. I have a stash of coloring books and some blocks there."

What he doesn't divulge is that they're there because his last Little boyfriend used to visit him in the office, something Ted absolutely adored. I know he misses being someone's Daddy as much as I did, but it's not a topic I push him on. He'll move forward when he's ready.

"I appreciate that," Ash replies, and we all know that he's not going to take Ted up on the offer. But I'm happy to know that, in an emergency, my best friend is there for my boy.

"Should we get burgers on the way home?" Ash asks, and I take that as my cue to give Ted back his space.

"Burgers sound fantastic."

Chapter Eleven — Asher

Charlie and I have our first actual fight three months into our relationship. I don't even know what starts it. One second, I'm asking him for his opinion on buying a new car now that I've got some savings behind me, and the next we're yelling at each other.

And, okay, maybe I do know what started it.

Because he constantly wants to buy me things and I hate being a leech.

"You're not a leech, you're my boyfriend!" He's seething, and a part of me finds this amusing because instead of fighting with negativity, he's yelling nice things at me.

But apparently smirking at him only makes him angrier.

"What the fuck is funny about that?"

I try to explain, but I can't get the words out for laughing.

Then he's laughing too, and then we're kissing, and...fight? What fight?

"Watching you all angry is fucking hot," I tell him, my hands scrabbling at his belt as he pushes me up against the nearest wall. "You get all loud and shouty and dominating…"

That's also something to think about. Even a month ago, having him angry and shouting at me would have left me a sobbing, anxious wreck. But between therapy and the night at Ted's, something has changed.

We always agreed to be equals in our relationship, but after that night, Charlie started confiding in me a bit more when he was struggling. And that made me feel like I was supporting him just as much as he was supporting me.

"You like me all dominating," he acknowledges, his voice rough. Probably from all the shouting. Or because I've just wrapped my hand around his cock.

"I do," I tell him with a shit-eating grin. "But sometimes I like to be a bit dominating, too."

He chuckles and his voice turns indulgent. "Bossy, maybe."

"Yeah, okay, I'll take that."

Charlie grinds into me, trying to get my hand to pump him. Because I have zero self-restraint, I do. "You'll take my cock" is his retort.

"Mmm," I hum in agreement. Then I nibble at his earlobe, feeling Big and bold enough to whisper, "but maybe one day you'll take mine?"

I am not anticipating that he'll come in my hand over that, but he does, swearing all the way.

"Holy fuck, Charlie." I laugh, wiping my hand on his underwear because he's already come in them. "What the hell?"

I mean, sure, it's been a few days since the last time either of us came, but that was still unexpected.

Charlie's not usually one to blush, but there's a pink tinge to his cheeks. "You kind of hit on something I've been thinking about for a little while, and I really liked it."

My lips curve into a knowing grin. "You don't say…"

"Shut up." He laughs, shaking his head. "But yeah, the idea of you fucking me is" —he gestures down to his pants— "that much of a turn-on."

"I'll remember that." The promise is full of heat, and we seal it with a kiss that reminds me I'm still hard as steel.

"Let Daddy take care of that," Charlie says, dropping to his knees in front of me. And I do.

* * *

Playdates have become a consistent element of my life now. Josh is still my favorite companion, but I have to admit that I tend to go deeper into my Little headspace when I'm with Emma or, surprisingly, Matt. Part of me occasionally wonders just how ridiculous it would look to an outsider to watch a forty-something, tattooed, biker-looking dude and some preppy, college-aged guy crawling around on the floor wearing diapers and sucking on pacifiers. But in Charlie's house it feels natural, and he always seems fondly amused to watch us play.

Matteo doesn't have a Daddy, but Charlie told him he's happy to be his caregiver during these playdates, too, which means Matt can be comfortable letting go and falling into his Little space. That makes me so proud of my Daddy. Whether he's doing it for me, or just because he's a natural caregiver, it doesn't matter. It's still selfless, because he and Matt don't have the sort of bond that he and I do, but he still kisses Matt's boo-boos, cuts up his meals, and cuddles him on his other side during story time.

"Your Daddy's the best," Matt says as we stack blocks in the corner of the living room.

I look over and smile at Charlie, because I know he's listening, even if he's pretending to read a grown-up book. "Yeah, he is."

"You're lucky," Matt replies, only now he seems sad. His voice goes all tight and crackly. "I miss my Daddy."

Uh-oh. I'm not good with tears. Especially not when I'm Little. I pat Matt's big back and try to comfort him. "You'll find a new Daddy," I say. Then I add, in case it's not already clear, "But not mine."

Charlie snorts and I look up again to frown at him. He's got his nose back in that book.

Hmm.

Matt's studying the yellow block in his hand like it has all the answers to life's problems. "I know. But if I could have a Daddy, I'd want one as nice as yours."

"I'm very lucky," I agree. I'm not super deep in Little space today, and I'm glad because I feel like Matt needs someone to talk to. Where I'm at right now seems to be just right. "Have you gone looking for a new Daddy?"

Mine just fell into my lap (or, rather, I guess I fell into his) but I know there are groups online, or munches, and The Grove apparently holds 'adoption' nights for unattached littles and caregivers to meet and mingle and play.

"I tried." Matt sighs and topples the tower we were building. "The last Daddy I met said I was too big and too old to be Little." He looks at the rug, his voice sounding smaller and more vulnerable than I've ever heard it before. Hurt seems to radiate from him. "They all do."

"Assholes."

Daddy pipes up from the couch, "Language, Ash."

Whoops.

Still, I'm kind of incensed right now; so instead of heeding the warning, I turn back to Matt. In my rage, I've slipped further out of my Little space, though I'm still not Big. Not with Matt still Little, too. "No, seriously, fuck that guy. Fuck them all."

"Asher!" Daddy's standing up now with his arms folded and a stern look on his face.

I pout. "But, Daddy…"

"What are the rules?" He holds firm.

Matt's looking between us with wide eyes because not many people get to hear Daddy's cranky voice. And usually, I don't push my luck with him. The last time was over not eating my peas —because, *eww, peas*— and I'd had to stand in the corner for five minutes. But this time, I'm too frustrated over the pain some random douche-canoe has caused my friend.

Ignoring Daddy, I turn back to Matt. "All those guys are fuckheads, and they're *wrong*."

"You've been warned, bud." Daddy's pulling me to my feet and marching me to the naughty corner. "*Ten* minutes."

I had cried over the pea thing, sniffling in the corner because I'd been bratty and I knew it. But this? Nope. I'm in the right.

I'm fidgeting after five minutes, but I'm not even close to feeling sorry for swearing.

At the ten-minute mark, when Daddy comes to ask me if I've thought about what I've done, I nod. But instead of apologizing like he expects, I fold my arms across my chest and say, "I'm not taking it back. The guys who said that to Matt can kiss my ass."

I'm pretty sure he looks amused for a moment —even a little proud— but then he schools his expression and says, "You'll be writing lines if you're not careful, Ash."

I roll my eyes. That's not going to change anything, and we

both know it.

"Asher." He sighs heavily, and now I start to wonder if maybe I shouldn't have been quite so bratty about it. "Whether I agree with your assessment or not, the rule is no swearing when you're Little."

Uh-oh. He's right.

"It's about behavior and limits. And I'm disappointed that you blatantly ignored me and continued to do the wrong thing. That sort of behavior isn't appropriate for little boys, and you shouldn't have said those words to Matteo while he was also Little, even if they weren't directed at him."

My brain is stuck on one word. *Disappointed? Oh no.*

Guilt begins to churn in my gut. He's never been disappointed in me. It hurts.

"Do you understand? I'm not happy with the way you chose to behave or the fact that you intentionally ignored me when I reminded you of the rules. You were deliberately naughty."

My sinuses sting with impending tears and my throat goes tight. I hate disappointing Daddy. Hate it. I want him to love me. I want him to be proud of me. My bottom lip quivers. I can't look him in the eye. The word "disappointed" is still echoing around my head.

"Oh, baby," he says softly, and then I lose it, flinging my arms around his neck and apologizing through heaving, messy sobs. It's been a long time since I last lost it like this.

When I tell him that I'm sorry for being a disappointment, he shakes his head next to mine. "That was a poor choice of words on my part, baby. *You* will never be a disappointment. The choices you made to break the rules and ignore me? Yeah. But *never* you." He holds me and rubs my back until I'm calm, and then surprises me by adding, "I'm sorry if I wasn't clear about why I was disciplining you, little lamb. And we'll talk about that properly when you're Big."

Communication is a big thing for Charlie. We ended up adding it as an afterthought to the honesty rule. It's important to him that we learn from any of these little struggles as we go, and I love how seriously he takes that — how seriously he takes *us*, whether I'm Little or big or somewhere in between.

* * *

Another addendum to the honesty rule? Lying by omission or deflection is still lying.

This isn't something we stumble upon through play. It's an issue that builds because I still find it difficult to voice the things I'm interested in trying. Like bottles. Charlie made it clear at the very beginning that he's waiting on me to set the pace for new experiences, and I appreciate that so much…but sometimes I just want him to make the decision for me.

We're wandering through Walmart the day after Matt's playdate. As we coast down the baby aisle Charlie asks, as he always does, if there's anything here I want. He watches me closely as my gaze flits to the bottles and then away.

I shrug. "I'm good."

He stops the cart and gives me *the look*. My dick stirs in my jeans because it's such a Daddy expression and it's fucking hot. When he pairs it with a low, warning-laden "Asher…" I need to shift my stance.

"I didn't ask if you were good," he adds, still not moving us further along the store. "I asked if there's anything you want."

My therapist, an awesome woman who has an intimate understanding of BDSM lifestyles, has been working with me to understand that there's nothing shameful in my kinks or interests. I'm a consenting adult with a supportive partner who wants all the same things I do. My fears and hang-ups, while totally normal, are just that: internal issues. Things I need to work through.

But I'm still struck by embarrassment as I stand here under the store's fluorescent lighting, even though there's nobody else in the aisle but Charlie and me.

Charlie's expression softens and he reaches for my hand, squeezing it. "You're my big, brave boy, remember. And I can't be the Daddy you need unless I know *what* you need."

His words help. This affirmation that he wants these things, too, but that he won't push for things that make me uncomfortable. As Ted says, it's a partnership. When I'm Little, I still have responsibilities in that role. Charlie's job is to take care of me, and mine is to let him know my needs. He's not a mind reader, even if sometimes I feel like that's what he's doing. I've just been good at giving him nonverbal cues.

"I…" I take a deep breath, then eye the bottles again. "Can we give bottles a try?"

Charlie's eyes light up, and he nods. "I have some at home," he informs me, and I'm not surprised. He squeezes my hand again. "What about a new toy?"

"You don't need to bribe me," I tease, but I reach for a set of bath paints that have grabbed my eye and he laughs, setting them in the cart and kissing the top of my head.

"It's a reward for being so brave."

I might roll my eyes, but the praise warms me from the inside. And later that afternoon, when I've been diapered and am snuggled up against Daddy on the couch, sucking milk through a bottle while he reads me a story before naptime, I feel like being brave is definitely worth it.

Chapter Twelve — Charlie

I can't stop thinking about Asher fucking me. We've spoken about it once —when I embarrassingly blew my load at the mere mention of it happening— but he hasn't brought it up again, and I don't want to push him.

Our sex life is definitely not lacking. We've been together almost four months now, and he's still like the freaking Energizer Bunny. But tonight, as we're rolling around the big king-size bed in the primary suite, playfully wrestling while we nip and tease with our mouths, I can't get the idea out of my head.

Our cocks slide against each other, drawing moans from each of us, and I give in and reach for the bedside table. It's another game we play: who's going to break and beg first. From where he's sucking a hickey into my clavicle, Ash chuckles.

"I knew it'd be you," he teases, then bites at my pec, knowing that it drives me wild when he gets a bit rough.

The thing about this game? Nobody ever loses.

I laugh and grind my erection into him, smearing precum

over his belly. "You cheated—you've been sending me sexy messages and making me hard all day." Thankfully, Max is a good enough partner not to say anything.

"Sorry not sorry." Ash squeezes my ass.

That's as good a cue as any for me to blurt, "So are you ever going to live up to your promise and fuck me?"

He freezes for a moment, then reaches for my bearded jaw so he can look me in the eye, all traces of playfulness gone. He's entirely an adult in this moment, and even though I adore all sides of him, this sharp, heated stare is incredibly sexy. "Are you sure you want that?"

I realize now that I haven't been fair to him. I've been reminding him over and over that if there's something he needs, he has to tell me…but I haven't given him the same courtesy in response.

"Ash," I tell him, my heart hammering in my chest, "I love you." He inhales sharply. We've danced around those words and have never said them. "I've loved you since… God, I think since I met you." I can't pinpoint the moment, but I started falling hard from the second I locked eyes on his beautiful hazel pair. "There's nothing I want more right now than to give you all of me and have all of you in return."

"I love you, too," he whispers, blinking back tears. It's a huge deal for him —for us— and I wait for him to process this new development.

He peppers kisses over my beard and cheeks before softly connecting our lips, slowly moving our tongues together as he lifts his hips up and rocks into me. We're both still hard and leaking, and the kiss goes from languorous to hot and heavy before too long.

When we part for air, his hands are back on my ass. "I've

never topped…" he confesses. "I won't last. Especially bare."

"It'll be perfect because it's you," I insist. "We don't need to set any world records tonight. Or ever."

"But I want it to be good for you and—"

"Baby, it will be." Then, for good measure I repeat, "Because. It's. You."

To get him out of his head, I kiss him again until the tension melts away from his shoulders. Then I roll us so I'm on my back and he's on top of me, and I press the bottle of lube I grabbed earlier into his hand. After sliding a pillow beneath my hips, Ash slicks his fingers and teases my hole with light, tentative touches at first, until I'm begging and bearing down on his finger.

It's not long before he's scissoring two inside me, and I have to breathe through the stretch and the burn. It's been a while —a long, long while— since I bottomed, but I need this. Need him. When the pain starts to ebb and give way to pleasure, my babbled begging starts up again and Ash smiles into the kiss he places on my lips.

"Can you take a third?"

"I'm gonna need to if you're going to fit," I answer, gasping as he crooks his fingers and brushes my prostate. "Jesus, Ash. Baby, more of that…"

He gives me exactly what I asked for, adds extra lube and then a third finger. By the time he deems me ready, I'm on the edge of coming. This might be his first time topping, but he clearly understands from experience what makes for enjoyable prep. Then he lubes his neglected cock up and strokes it a few times, putting on a show just for me, before notching the head at my entrance. He stares down at me with laser focus as he inches in. Once he's made it past the tight ring of muscles and

I've breathed through the additional burn, he sinks inside me slowly with short, smooth thrusts of his hips.

"You're so fucking tight and hot," he says through gritted teeth. "Daddy...*fuck*..." He bottoms out and stills, breathing hard. "You're amazing." He leans down, with his hands planted on the mattress on either side of my shoulders, and kisses my chest, then asks, "You okay?"

"Uh-huh," I answer, feeling full and loved and a little over-whelmed. "I'm good. Just...move when you're ready." I want to demand that he start moving, but he's still my boy and I'm not forcing him if he needs more time.

Above me, Ash sets his jaw and starts rocking his hips languidly.

It feels so fucking good.

"Charlie..." He exhales after a few thrusts. "*Daddy*, I'm already so close..." He's still moving, though, and he shifts his angle experimentally and I see stars for a moment as he grazes that magical spot inside me.

"Do that again and I'll beat you there," I growl out, grabbing his hips and fucking up onto him, trying to find that angle again.

It takes a little maneuvering, but when he gets it I shout, opening my eyes again to catch him grinning at me.

Then he bends and we kiss sloppily.

"Fuck, I love this," he says against my mouth, our panting breaths mingling. "I love you. So much."

"Me too," I murmur, before he rests his weight on one elbow to reach between us and pump my cock in time with his movements. "Oh, Ash, baby, yes..."

He speeds up and we're both close, our breathing ragged, sweat slicking our skin. When his cock brushes my prostate again, I don't even have time to warn him before I'm coming hard over our abdomens and his hand, which is milking rope after rope of cum from me.

I'm still riding the wave of pleasure when I realize that my orgasm has pulled him over the edge with me, his hips jerking. I feel the heat of his release inside me, dribbling out of my ass when he pulls out as gently as he can. It's messy, and sticky, and cooling…and absolutely perfect.

"Shower?" he asks, having flopped down on the mattress beside me to catch his breath.

I turn my head, feeling boneless and sleepy, and kiss his shoulder. "Definitely."

And, when we get out of the shower and he starts slipping into his Little headspace, I'm once again overwhelmed by just how perfect he is for me.

* * *

I call my parents to tell them all about Asher the next day. It's something I've been putting off because Mom can be…*a lot*. I know I've gotten my caregiver tendencies from her, but she's loud and excitable and will probably try to smother Ash with adoration. Don't get me wrong: he deserves all the love in the world. But he's also kind of skittish, and my mother might just scare him off.

Still, we've officially exchanged I-love-yous now, and I have no reason to hide him from my family. In fact, I want to show him off, this beautiful man of mine.

When Mom picks up the phone, I can't help but smile at her infectious joy. "Well, if it isn't my firstborn," she answers, and I can picture the shit-eating grin on her face. "You finally remembered that you have parents, huh?"

"I texted you last week." I sigh dramatically, deliberately poking the bear.

"You sent a thumbs up when I texted to say hi."

"I can move on to GIFs instead of emojis if you'd like?"

"That does feel much more personalized."

I laugh and so does she, and I do have to acknowledge that I miss her, even if she does get a little suffocating sometimes. My dad's the calming influence, but he generally lets her do what she wants because it's easier and he likes to indulge her. Now that I've got Ash in my life, I can understand that more.

"So, how much money do you need?" Mom jokes. "Or do we finally need to bail you out of jail?"

"You're hilarious, Mom," I deadpan, and I lean back in my desk chair at the station. I've finished my shift, but I want to have this conversation where Ash can't hear. Not because I have anything to hide from him, but because it's a private moment for me. "How's that career in stand-up comedy working out for you?"

"Getting defensive?" she teases back. We honestly could do this all day. She snickers. "Oh, I know, this is finally the Oops-my-girlfriend-is-pregnant call! Tell me, how far along is she?"

I don't miss a beat, not taking the bait and instead turning it on her. "Just wait; Axel's gonna give you that call one day for sure."

Her gasp is dramatic, and I can imagine her pressing a hand to her chest, clutching at imaginary pearls. My mom's a bit of a drama queen. "You wash your mouth out with soap. My baby's a responsible boy."

I can't resist. "...For now." He's only eighteen. He's got time to prove her wrong.

"I'll tell him that his big brother has zero faith in him."

"Oh, don't worry; I text him that on a daily basis. Gotta keep his ego in check."

We both know that's a lie. I adore my youngest sibling. Mom's right: he can do no wrong.

"You're a terror," she accuses with another laugh. "Now, are you actually going to tell your poor, old mother why you called out of the blue, or do I have to keep guessing?"

I take a steadying breath, allowing the din of the station to fade into the background. Phones ringing, people talking, the guy at the desk to my left slurping his sludgy station-brew coffee…it all ceases to exist. "I'm in love, Mom. His name's Asher, we've been together for a few months…and I'm crazy about him."

It feels so good to say it out loud. Especially to my mother. I joke about how insane she makes me, but she's honestly the person whose opinion matters most to me. When I was growing up, she was my rock. Keeping Ash from her, and from the rest of my family, feels wrong on so many levels.

I know I should have said something earlier, but there was a part of me that worried it might not work out…and then life got busy, and I didn't prioritize telling them. That makes me feel guilty. But, to be fair, I've never done this before. I've never been serious enough with anyone to feel like I needed to tell them. Is four months too late? Not early enough?

What's done is done now, but…maybe I should have called sooner.

In the silence that follows my blurted confession, I check the screen of my phone to make sure the call is still connected. Then I start to get anxious. "Mom?"

"Oh, Charlie." She sniffles, which takes me completely by surprise. "I'm so happy for you."

Relief sweeps through me and my shoulders sag.

Then the torrent of questions comes down the line. Mom's voice escalates in pitch and speed as her excitement ramps up. "When can we meet him? Dinner tonight? Tomorrow? You can bring him over and I'll take care of everything. What's his favorite food? Does he have any allergies?"

Midway through her stream-of-consciousness style interrogation, I try to interrupt. "Mom…"

She steamrolls right over me. "Oh, would it be easier for your dad and I to come to you? You're probably tired from working so hard. Asher, that's such a sweet name. Tell me everything about him."

"Mom…"

"Is he younger than you? You've always liked them a bit younger, haven't you? Not that that's a problem. As long as you're both consenting adults and you're being safe, you know Dad and I won't judge you—"

"Jesus Christ, Mom." I facepalm and wonder why I decided to make this call in public. I know that nobody else can hear her, but I'm limited by how I can respond. "*Stop*. Just…stop."

I can understand her enthusiasm, though. This is the first time since high school that I've directly told her about one of my relationships. She's bound to know how serious it is for that reason alone. Additionally, she's only ever wanted her kids to be as disgustingly happy as she and Dad are. The funny thing is, I think Ash and I are, and I can see us staying that way. I've never thought that before. Not about my previous relationships, I mean. But with Ash, I can imagine forever with him. It should scare me, but it doesn't.

To be honest, it thrills me that my mom is as excited about my news as I am, even if I don't ramble on.

Not out loud, anyway.

"You're going to introduce us soon, right?"

"Of course, but…"

"But?! I know you're not ashamed of your mother, Charles Franklin Walker." I can picture her narrowing her eyes at me, and it makes me squirm even though she's a forty-five-minute drive away.

"Oh, I got the full name treatment." I try to verbally sidestep, not having thought this entire plan through. Because of course Mom's not going to accept the news that I've fallen in love without demanding to meet Ash instantly.

"*Charlie.*" She's got her Mom voice down pat. It's very Domme. I'm pretty sure it's where I learned to sound like such a stern Daddy.

"Okay, so, here's the thing…" I begin, hoping that I can calm her down so I can prepare Ash for the insanity that is my family. "Ash has been through a lot, and he's a bit…anxious about meeting new people. I'd like to ease him into the concept of meeting you guys."

"Ease him in?" Mom sounds insulted. "We're not going to mob the poor boy."

I remember exactly how she handled meeting my first boyfriend, and I scoff. "You can come on a bit strong at first is all I'm saying."

It takes a lot of convincing, but she eventually promises to wait until I'm ready to introduce them to the man I've fallen in love with. I just hope that she'll keep that promise. You never know with my mom, and it's best to be prepared for anything.

I'll broach the subject with Ash soon, but for now I'm content with having him to myself.

Chapter Thirteen – Asher

"Asher?" I freeze at the voice behind me. It's not one I thought I'd hear again, and it's not one I ever wanted to, either.

It's a Saturday, but Charlie and Josh are both working, so I decided to go shopping, formulating a plan in my head to surprise Charlie by cooking him dinner for once. The last time I'd wanted to do this, my car broke down. Maybe these are all signs from the universe that cooking for my Daddy is not in the cards for me.

"Asher." The voice is getting closer and it's just as gruff and unhappy as the last time I heard it. "Don't ignore me."

The urge to slip into my Little headspace to avoid the confrontation and stress is strong, but in this situation it'll only make things worse. With a deep breath, I square my shoulders and turn to face the person whose voice I least want to hear.

"Dad." I address him simply. No hello. No fake smile. No indication that I have any actual interest in talking to him. But I don't sound upset, either, which is something.

At least we're in public. He won't make a scene in public.
I hope.

He stops a few feet away from me, not the towering, fearsome figure from my memories any longer. He's still taller than me, still imposing and larger than life, but he doesn't inspire terror in me now. Maybe because he doesn't have any power over me. He can't threaten the roof over my head or my college degree anymore.

Dad looks me up and down with a sneer. "You landed on your feet, then?"

It shouldn't hurt. It shouldn't. But the implication that he was hoping that I wouldn't recover eats away at me. What kind of parent wants their kid to suffer? What did he hope would happen to me when he kicked me out? Actually, no, I don't want to know.

Folding my arms across my chest, I nod curtly. "I did." I refuse to give him any information. He's not going to learn about Charlie, or the friends I've made, or the job I've landed, or the plans I have to finish my degree after all.

"You disgust me," Dad says, leaning in to deliver the assessment. He's repeating some of the awful things he said the day he unknowingly set me free, and while the words hurt, I'm surprised that the voice in my head which once agreed with him is telling me he's wrong. Leaning closer to me, he spits out, "How can you stand there and look so proud of yourself? It's bad enough you were queer," he sneers the word like a slur, "but the freaky shit is beyond the pale. They should lock you up for that pedophile crap."

I feel myself blanch, but before I can refute him, I'm interrupted by a much more welcome voice.

"Ash." A large, tattooed arm slings around my shoulders and I sag into Matt's side. He's come out of nowhere, but I'm beyond relieved to have the support. I turn my head and crane my neck. He's looking down at me with concern and his phone is in his hand. "Is this guy giving you grief? Should I call Charlie?" He eyes my dad warily. "You know, your cop boyfriend?"

I'm guessing he was close enough to catch at least the tail end of my father's vitriol. A part of me curls in on itself. The thought of Matt hearing my father talk to me that way is beyond embarrassing. I feel genuine shame coursing through my veins.

"Fuck off," Dad hisses, not seeming to care that Matt's built like a linebacker and could probably lay him out with one punch. He also seems to have ignored the implicit threat of my dating a cop. The asshole always did think he was above the law. "This is between me and my son."

Matt's arm tenses around my shoulders and I know the jigsaw puzzle that is me and my anxiety issues is all falling into place for him.

But it's me that speaks, and I put this sudden burst of confidence down to my therapy and Charlie. "I stopped being your son when you kicked me out and left me homeless and alone." It feels so good to get this closure. Like a weight is being lifted from my shoulders. The albatross around my neck removed. And because I'm giddy and can't help myself from stirring the pot, I lean forward conspiratorially and tell him, "But because you did that, I found my Daddy and I've never been happier. So, really, maybe I should thank you for that. You did me a solid."

I offer him a sharp, shit-eating grin before I turn away, leaving him red-faced and sputtering, and Matt chortles at my side. "Holy shit, dude." He gives me an excited little shake, even though I'm starting to tremble as the shock of what the fuck I just did sets in. "That was incredible!"

My answering smile feels tremulous, but I'm aware that I've just had some sort of breakthrough. I mean, I just told the bigot that booted me out of my house that I have a Daddy. I said it in public. With pride. And I meant everything I said.

"Charlie's going to be so proud of you."

Except Daddy's also going to be worried. He's going to hate that I goaded my father. That I wasn't the bigger man, and that I didn't just walk away. I still let Dad's crap get under my skin, and who knows what that's going to do to my recovery from the trauma. Is it going to set me back? Are the nightmares —which have become few and far between— going to start back up again?

It's too late to voice any of this, though, because Matt's already typed out a text to Charlie. He's probably concerned that I've gone a little catatonic beside him. And though he's a strong, capable man when he's Big, he still doesn't have the Daddy vibes I need to settle my burst of anxiety.

"Where've you parked?" he asks me after what I assume is a reply from Charlie.

I rally enough to answer, "I caught the bus." I still haven't bought a new car, and I didn't want to risk mine dying again. "I was only going to buy a few things."

He taps away on his phone screen again, then slides it into his pocket and takes me to his car. He drives a white, late-model sedan, and I have a private laugh that it's not a motorcycle. His look screams "biker," but I know better than anyone not to stereotype. It's only as I'm buckling myself in that I start to come back to reality.

"Didn't you need to buy anything?"

Matt shakes his head. "Nothin' that can't wait."

I accept his words at face value, acknowledging that I'd do the same for him in a heartbeat, and let him drive me home. He hangs around and we talk about everything and nothing —how our fantasy football leagues are doing, our thoughts on the most recent NHL draft, who the best character on *Once Upon A Time* was— and by the time Charlie walks through the door, I'm pretty much back to my usual self.

Charlie claps Matt on the back and thanks him as he goes to leave, and I hug him and do the same. He shrugs our thanks off with a sheepish grin and leaves, and once again I find myself musing on how lucky I am to have stumbled into a life with these people. Charlie and his friends have become my found family. And having just faced the last of my biological family, I know that the grass is definitely greener on this side of the fence.

"You okay, baby?" Charlie asks me once he's closed the door. He's holding my face in his hands and looking me over as though I'd gotten into a physical fight.

I smile brightly at him. "I've never been better."

It's not even a lie.

* * *

It turns out that getting closure with my father was something I desperately needed. It was kind of like I had to physically face my fears, and once I did, all that self-loathing and those fears of being abnormal and embarrassed about what I wanted started to fall away faster.

It wasn't instantaneous, not by a long shot. But after publicly telling my asshole father that I'd found a Daddy, it's been easier with each passing day to tell Charlie when I need something.

"Daddy, I need cuddles." "Daddy, I want a bottle." "Daddy, play blocks with me." "Daddy, help me potty." "Daddy, I'm horny."

Okay, so that last one has always come pretty easily to me.

But every time I vocalize my needs, I watch Daddy's eyes light up and he tells me I'm a good boy. Nothing feels better than that. We even start going out to The Grove on Littles' Nights.

The club turns out to be nothing like the dingy, oppressive space I'd imagined. Instead, it's a huge warehouse space on the edge of the city, heading into the industrial part of town. It's unassuming from the outside, with its entrance on the side of the building: a plain black door with an olive tree imprinted on it.

The room we enter when we step inside is bright and kind of bland. It reminds me of the waiting room at my childhood dentist's office. There's a pretty woman working the counter, and she looks like a sexy librarian in her pencil skirt, blouse, and cat-eye glasses.

Charlie's a member and she greets him by name, handing over a selection of colored paper wristbands which he fastens to his right wrist. Then she turns to me.

"And you must be Ash," she says cheerily. "Your Daddy called to book you for tonight's session. Has he run through the rules?"

I nod because Charlie has been very thorough about the club's nondisclosure agreement, the house safe word (monitored electronically and by the moderators in each room), the whole "flagging" thing (hence his wristbands) and the sorts of things to expect once we're inside. I'm nervous but excited.

She beams and asks me to sign the NDA she's prepared.

When Charlie called ahead to book us for the event, he gave all of my details ahead of time, so I don't need to fill in a temporary membership application for the night — though I do have to sign it, and the indemnity waivers, too. I hand over my ID and she passes me my wristbands to indicate my preferences. Charlie helps me put them on. After she makes sure I know the house safe word ("turmeric"), she sends us through the two large metal doors on the far side of the room.

Once we pass through those, my jaw drops.

There must be significant soundproofing around the building, because the bass and general wave of sound from the music pumping into the large, open nightclub space in front of us is intense. There's a bar and a dance floor and dimly lit booths lining the walls. There's also an elevated stage at the far end of the space, and Charlie's already told me that they host scenes and demonstrations here.

There's a wide hallway that surrounds the club space, traveling around the entire building. It leads to the locker rooms and bathrooms, as well as the back staircase and elevators to the second floor, which is host to the playrooms. That's where we're heading.

We ride the elevator to the second floor, and it feels like a hotel up here. Two parallel hallways greet us, and the one we walk down is lined with doors to rooms Charlie says are themed playrooms. The other hallway is apparently the same. These spaces can be booked for specific scenes, and Charlie points out a couple as we walk past. There's a classroom, a corporate office and boardroom, and a sauna. Then there's the space we want: the littles' playroom.

When we walk in, I blink. It's a massive, brightly lit space, full of color and toys and everything a Little could want. It

111

looks like it runs the entire width of the warehouse building and takes up at least a quarter of the top floor.

"Holy shit," I breathe, staring with wide eyes as the door closes behind us. "Is that a bouncy castle?"

It's at the far end of the space, taking up the bulk of the end of the room from ceiling to floor. It looks like it can only hold three or four adults comfortably at a time, but it's definitely a freaking bouncy castle.

"Yep," Charlie acknowledges. "Wanna bounce?"

I itch to, but I shake my head. Tonight, I'm not comfortable being Little. I just want to see what this place is all about. I look around a bit more.

Couches line the wall to my left, presumably for Mommies and Daddies who want to watch their littles play. In the middle of the carpeted floor, there are mats and rugs and buckets of toys. To my right, there's a massive train set, beanbags, and brightly colored tables laden with paints and crayons and markers. It's like a giant day care center...with a bouncy castle.

"There's a changing room across the hall," Charlie says. "Did you want to see that, too?"

I shake my head again. "I'm imagining it's like a giant nursery? Changing tables and all that jazz?"

"Pretty much."

"Good to know."

We're the first to arrive tonight, and I'm not wearing my Little clothes. I just wanted to see what the place was like. Charlie doesn't push me, and we settle into a corner as a group of littles and their caregivers enter the room, laughing and chatting.

For this first time, I'm too shy to do more than sit in a corner and watch the other littles play and participate in the evening's organized activities.

On the second Littles' Night we attend, I ask Daddy to dress me in my training pants, a onesie, and some play shorts. I join Josh, Matt, and Emma in some finger painting (which leads to an awesome bath time experience later that night because I *accidentally* manage to get paint *everywhere*).

On the third visit, I'm in another onesie, this time wearing a diaper I'm still not ready to use; but I'm playing with littles I've never met, and interacting with Mommies and Daddies that aren't Charlie or his friends.

This is when I finally realize that there is nothing shameful in my kinks. Most people have *something* that makes them tick, and to be ashamed of what I share with Charlie —with my Daddy— is unfair to him and to our relationship. I'm still not going to walk down the street broadcasting our lifestyle, but I no longer panic at the thought of someone discovering that I'm kinky, although the kink I'm into is sometimes looked down on even by others in the BDSM community, which I think is ridiculous.

When I see her next, my therapist says this is a huge breakthrough for me, and I suppose she's right. This is who I am, and I'm happy to embrace it.

So it's no surprise that, the next time Daddy has Ted and Chance over for beers and grown-up time, I'm beyond comfortable being Little. I'm kind of disappointed that Spencer and Emma couldn't make it, and that Josh and Matt had other plans, but I'm not disappointed enough to hide this part of me from the others. It's not like it's the first time they've seen me in Little space, anyway. It's become more and more regular, especially when they tend to visit at random. The fact that they're involved in the lifestyle helps, too.

Daddy and his friends are on the couch talking while I'm sprawled on my stomach on the play mat in front of them, kicking my socked feet back and forth in the air behind me. I'm thoroughly entertained by the water mat Ted bought me on a whim. It's like finger painting without the mess, and I'm mesmerized by it. I lose myself in play, and it's the deepest I've *ever* been into my Little space, to the point where I don't even notice just how far gone I am. It's glorious. It feels like complete freedom from my adult responsibilities and worries. I play, and I giggle, and I've tuned out everything Daddy and his friends are saying.

Every so often, one of them asks me to show them my latest picture, or joins me to play with a different toy for a while, or hands me a snack or my sippy cup; but they're all just as content to let me float in my happy space as I am to do it. It's a magical afternoon.

I'm so far into Little space that I don't even notice how badly I need to pee until I sit up. Lying on my stomach has dulled the urge and distracted me from needing to potty, but as soon as I'm vertical, gravity's not my friend. I'm on my knees, but as soon as I move one leg out to try to stand, my bladder gives way a bit.

I go straight back to my knees and bite my lip.

I'm diapered, as I happen to be more often than not when I'm in my Little space nowadays, but up to this point it's been a comfort thing. And that's probably part of how I got so far into Little space this time, really. I've let go and embraced my Little urges completely because I felt safe and relaxed.

Besides, Daddy's made it clear that he's got no issues when I do wet my diaper, or even if I have accidents in my training pants — I know that's *never* going to happen, because the thought of deliberately pushing that envelope when I'm a bigger Boy doesn't appeal; however, I've been good with the status quo. I'll admit that I have been curious to the point where we've both started saying "when" I use my diaper, not "if", but I've still never been in the right headspace to just let go and try.

Today, though, I've let myself get there...and it's not scary.

I know I could try and crawl to the bathroom, but I decide not to. I decide to just let go. And when it happens, I'm not hit with the panic or feeling of wrongness that I'd expected this moment would bring.

Instead, aside from the relief I feel as my bladder empties into the absorbent material, I feel the strangest surge of absolute freedom and a tiny bit of curious excitement. Maybe there is a mild bit of humiliation kink somewhere deep in my psyche, too. I know public humiliation isn't my thing, but maybe a bit of embarrassment in front of my Daddy does give me a thrill after all. Who knows? Either way, I know that Daddy's got this. He's going to change me, and it's going to be just another thing we do together. I trust him completely.

Was I planning on having this revelation with two other Daddies in the same room? No. But I'm not worried.

"Hey little lamb." Daddy's voice startles me because it's much closer than where he's been sitting on the couch. He's crouching beside me, his head tilted to the side, his blue eyes warm but cautious. "You okay? You've been sitting here really still for a minute."

I turn into him, hiding my face in his neck. "Daddy..." I whine because the situation in my diaper is now weighty, a bit damp, and becoming noticeably uncomfortable.

He rubs my back. "What's wrong, baby?"

115

Even though I know he's not going to react badly, the part of my brain that's still an adult knows that we haven't discussed this recently. The last time we did, I said I'd let him know when I felt ready.

I've blown past giving him the heads-up that it was potentially going to happen, haven't been able to warn him that I was ready today. And as my headspace clears with that knowledge, a tiny bit of embarrassment sneaks in after all. Maybe I should have waited until it was just the two of us? Too late now.

Burrowing my face farther into him and feeling my cheeks burn, I whisper, "I... Daddy, I... I *wet*."

Daddy doesn't miss a beat, but I imagine he's a little surprised —I'm sure he didn't think this would happen with company around, either— and his hand sneaks between us to pat the front of my diaper through the onesie. It's not a sexual touch, but I feel a short thrill of some convoluted, bubbly feeling at the action anyway.

"So you are," he observes, and I can hear him smiling. "You're such a good boy for telling me." Then he's pulling me to my feet and telling the others we'll be back in a minute.

Ted and Chance are both Daddies, too, and neither even blinks at the situation. It's perfectly normal to them, and my momentary embarrassment fades.

This is when I discover that walking in a heavy, wet diaper is not fun. I'm waddling worse than usual, and the sensation against my skin is not pleasant. Climbing the stairs is even worse, and I cringe my way through it.

Daddy spreads a towel out on the bed in my little boy room and then *lifts me* onto it, gently arranging me onto my back. That's new, too, but I kind of love the casual display of his strength, and the way it seems to affirm my littleness. "Baby,

I'm so, *so* proud of you," Daddy tells me as he undoes the snaps holding the short legs of my onesie together. "I know this was a huge deal for you, and I love that you trust me so much to explore it."

And I do. I trust him implicitly. But I'm still feeling too Little to express that properly. All I can do is smile, wriggle my hips, and say, "Change now?"

The blinding smile he shoots me in return takes away any vestiges of awkwardness.

Yeah, I think as I lie back and Daddy wipes and changes me with efficiency, as though we've been doing this all along. *Daddy's got this.*

* * *

"Little lamb." Daddy kisses my neck after bath time, making me giggle. I'm wrapped in my towel, nice and dry, but his hands are still traveling over my body. "You were such a good boy today."

After Chance and Ted left, I took a nap, feeling oddly emotional after taking that final leap. Daddy napped with me, holding me close. I wondered if he was just as affected as I was. I got the feeling that the answer was yes.

When we woke up, Daddy took me out for dinner. I was Big, as I always am when we're in public, but for the first time I asked him to order for me, testing the waters for potentially slipping into Little habits more often. The surprised delight in his eyes was worth it. Plus, he ordered me a steak with mushroom sauce —my favorite— instead of something off the kid's menu, which I found relief in. We were still equals on our date, even if I was giving him a little more control. Still balanced and still in sync. It was just what I had needed after the afternoon's events.

I might have teased Daddy a little during the meal as a reward for just how perfect he had been. Between my hand inching up his thigh and the indecent way I treated every bite of food on my fork, I had watched as his pupils had dilated and his grip on his own cutlery had tightened. But it was my moans over the decadent chocolate mousse I'd ordered for dessert which had done him in.

Daddy had rushed us out of that restaurant so fast, I'd wanted to call him the Flash. But instead of pinning me against the car and kissing me senseless, he'd been a gentleman. Conversation on the drive home had remained just as easy as it had been over dinner, even though I could see the outline of his cock straining in his jeans. Mine was equally hard.

Daddy still didn't have his way with me when we got home, though. He'd just pinched my ass and told me it was bath time...and had restrained himself during all of that, too. Even washing my body with the washcloth, he didn't linger on my cock or play with my hole.

It took a while for me to realize that he was holding himself back to "punish" me. The sneaky bastard.

But now that I've been toweled off and I've slipped back into Little space, his touches have turned playful and naughty.

My cock is aching for him, leaking precum while he continues to avoid it. The only thing keeping me from complaining is the feel of his own hard length poking into my back through the layers of his clothes.

His words finally register in my brain. I was a good boy today. This is both a "punishment" for the restaurant and a reward for putting my trust in him, and I'm simultaneously hating and loving every second of it.

"*Daddy...*" I gasp as his tongue travels over the shell of my ear. "Daddy, I *need...*"

The towel falls, landing with a muted thud as it crumples on the mat at my feet. Some of the steam from my bath is still lingering in the air, warming the bathroom and fogging the glass of the mirror above the basin, so I can't see our reflections in it beyond the blur of our shapes.

"What do you need, little lamb?" Daddy's whisper is husky in my ear and my cock jumps, eliciting a deep chuckle that vibrates through me because his chest is pressed against my back.

"*Daddy...*"

I feel his lips curve into a smile against the skin of my jaw. "You need Daddy to take care of this?" His hand finally grasps my aching shaft and his thumb smooths over the head, smearing precum everywhere. I buck into his palm, nodding enthusiastically.

"*Please.*"

"What else do you need, baby boy?"

My brain is mush. Words are too difficult. I whine.

Daddy trails wet, open-mouthed kisses down my neck and into the hollow of my throat from behind me, the hair of his beard scratching and tickling in the best ways. "I need you to tell me, Asher."

Fuck, that authoritative tone is the hottest thing ever. He knows what it does to me. Especially when I'm floating in Little space.

Bending over, I push my ass back at him, grinding against his insanely hard bulge. "Inside me, Daddy."

His hands move to my ass cheeks, fondling them, squeezing

them, spreading them. A dry finger trails down my crack, teases my hole. "In here?"

"Please. *Please, please, please.*"

Daddy stills. "Please, *what?*"

I swear to God, I'm going to come without even touching myself if he keeps using that tone. "Please, *Daddy.*"

"Good boy."

More precum dribbles from my tip and slides down my raging erection, but I know I can't stroke myself. I'm never allowed to when I'm Little. It's one of Daddy's rules. A whimper escapes me and I push back against his hand, trying to coerce him into teasing me again.

I almost cry when he takes the hand away completely. He laughs and smacks my ass lightly, a sign to get moving. "I don't have any lube in here, baby. Let's go to our room, okay?"

He doesn't need to tell me twice. I scamper out of the bathroom and across the carpeted living space, down the short hallway that leads to the primary suite. I dig out the lube from the bedside table and hold it out with both my arms extended in childlike glee as Daddy saunters through the bedroom door at a more sedate pace, those big fingers of his working the buttons of his sexy dress shirt.

He looks every bit a Daddy tonight. Pressed black trousers and a sky-blue dress shirt rolled to his elbows, a little damp and ruffled from having given me a bath. His blue eyes are dark with desire when he looks at me. Even though we've been together for months, the sight of him still takes my breath away.

"I love you, Daddy," I blurt out, unprompted.

His expression softens and he steps forward, abandoning his shirt buttons to kiss me sweetly. "I love you, too, little lamb."

My heart flutters as it always does when he says those words. After today, they seem even stronger somehow. Cemented by my absolute trust in him.

Our mouths meet again, and I lick at the seam of his lips, silently begging to deepen the connection. Daddy opens for me and our tongues dance together. His strong arms pull me flush against him as he takes over, dominating the kiss. I wriggle my hands between us, clumsily trying to undo his shirt, pulling away to cheer in victory when the fabric parts to reveal Daddy's muscular abdomen.

He laughs and takes half a step back, pulling his rolled-up sleeves back down to his wrists so I can push the shirt over his big, strong shoulders. The material slides off his arms and to the floor, then my hands fumble with Daddy's belt buckle.

"I've got this," he tells me, sounding amused when I make a sound of frustration at the back of my throat. He shoots me a smoldering look. "Get on the bed. On your hands and knees — butt up, head down."

I scramble to obey, climbing into position in the middle of the mattress and listening to the sounds of him shedding the rest of his clothing. The bed moves as he climbs on behind me and I shiver with anticipation at the feel of his big hands on my ass cheeks.

Instead of reaching for the lube I've helpfully left near my leg, Daddy spreads me open and I feel his hot breath ghosting over my hole. Swallowing convulsively, I wait for what's coming. He doesn't disappoint and I gasp at the warm, wet sensation of his tongue licking a stripe from my balls and over my taint before he teases my entrance.

I start babbling incoherently when he finally works his tongue inside me, spearing it in and out in a maddeningly slow rhythm. My cock is painfully hard now, leaking profusely, and I rock back against Daddy's face, not getting nearly enough stimulation out of the tongue-fucking, but not wanting it to stop, either. He works his tongue with practiced ease, loosening me up while he eats me out.

I start begging, completely lost to the exquisite torture of this experience, and I cry out when he pulls away to finally grab the lube.

"Easy, baby; Daddy's got you." His words are soothing, but his voice is tight with his own intense need. Thankfully, he doesn't drag the prep out further, but he praises me while he works two —and then three— fingers in. "You were so brave for me today, Ash. So brave, and your trust in me is so fucking hot. What you do to me…"

I can barely process the words, too horny to properly understand that he's talking about this afternoon. I moan loudly when he finally buries his cock inside me with one smooth push of his hips.

"My good boy." He pulls back out and thrusts in deep again, then leans over me, covering my body with his to snake his hand underneath us and grab my weeping dick. Then he tugs me up into a kneeling position, still pumping into me, holding me upright with my back to his chest and his other arm wrapped possessively around my front.

He uses my precum and the remnants of lube from slicking himself up to glide his hand up and down my length. Ecstasy bubbles beneath my skin while he brings his mouth to my ear again. "My sweet, perfect little lamb. I love you so much."

Oh, my heart.

"*Daddy*, I—" I don't even finish the warning. With a twist of his wrist on an upstroke and his cock brushing my prostate, I fly over the edge of my orgasm, coming so hard I think I white out for a moment.

When my brain reengages, Daddy's crying out his own release, holding me tightly while his cock swells and spurts inside me. It's perfect. Everything about today has been perfect.

We're panting, catching our breaths, and a giggle bursts from my lips. "Daddy," I complain playfully, "you got me all dirty again."

He snorts and presses a tired kiss to the sensitive spot behind my ear. "Are you really complaining, baby?"

"Nope."

Not now, not ever. I have lucked out with this man, and I know it.

Chapter Fourteen — Charlie

"You've got a spring in your step today," Max says with a laugh as we start our new shift. We've had the weekend off, which happens once a month, and we're on the early beat this week. It's ridiculously early —barely six a.m.— but I'm on cloud nine because life is good.

My boyfriend finally felt comfortable enough to tick the last thing off the list of Little experiences he had wanted to try; I know it sounds ridiculous to be so excited about that, but it was such a big deal for him. I don't have the words for how proud I am of him, or how humbled I am that he trusted me enough to finally let go and slide so deeply into Little space, but it meant everything to me. And seeing him so happy and confident as a Little only makes me happier.

Once Asher was Big again, I showed him just how happy he made me. The additional orgasms late into the night —and the quick blow jobs we exchanged this morning— are worth how tired I am now. Thank God for caffeine.

"Life is good, Max," I answer my partner as we walk away

from our lockers and check in with the departing shift.

He chuckles and shakes his head. "And when am I gonna meet this boy of yours, then?"

I falter in my step because he says "boy" like it's more than just *boyfriend*. And even though I don't care if he knows about my kinks, I know Ash is still hoping to keep it in the family, so to speak. He doesn't call me Daddy when we're on dates, and he doesn't slip into his Little headspace when we're out, either. And that's fine with me. It works for us.

Max claps me on the back. "I'm a cop, Charlie. And you're not subtle."

"Look, I don't care if you know," I tell him as I fall into step with him, "but Ash is…"

"Private." He finishes for me, sweeping his blond hair back off his forehead. "I get it. *Trust me.*"

I arch an eyebrow, but he doesn't elaborate. I've never seen him at The Grove, but that doesn't mean he's not kinky. Besides, The Grove isn't the only fetish club in the city, though it is the best for a number of reasons. It's exclusive, there's a vetting process for members, and all members must sign NDAs to attend. It's the safest space of its kind for people in the kink community. However, instead of pressing my partner for more information, I nod and go back to his original question. "He'd love to meet you, too."

It's not a lie. Ash has mentioned wanting to meet my "work husband" a few times now. He's proud of his nickname for Max, and I know there's not even a hint of jealousy behind it.

"So is there a reason you're keeping us apart? I mean, aside from the stuff I'm not supposed to know about?"

I roll my eyes at the teasing lilt to his voice. "I get it, subtlety is not my strong suit." We bump into the guys we're taking over for and exchange notes and pleasantries. As they walk away, I explain, "It's just been a hectic few months. I promise you'll get to meet him soon."

"I'm sure I'm gonna love him," Max replies as we slide into our seats in the patrol car. "How can I not, when he's the reason you've got that goofy-ass grin on your face most days?"

"Shut up," I say with a laugh. "Maybe I'm just this happy 'cause the Piranhas beat the Tigers?" I say, referencing our NHL teams who played a preseason game against each other over the weekend.

"That was sheer luck and a bad call from the ref." Max takes the bait, and we launch into a lighthearted debate over the game.

* * *

Things start going south near the end of our shift. It's early afternoon, and we're called to check out a robbery in progress because we're the closest unit to the scene. When we get to the jewelry store in question, there are three perps in masks and a handful of terrified store staff in what I can only call a hostage situation. The perps freak out the second they notice us in our uniforms.

There's yelling and gunfire before we can fall back and call for backup. A searing pain in my chest is surpassed only by the matching pain in my right thigh.

Then the world goes black.

Chapter Fifteen — Asher

"Josh." I smile, surprised as the man in question walks through to the admin team.

A couple of the women titter, and I hear Louise whisper "Hot damn" under her breath. I can't say I blame them. Like his older brother, Josh Walker is a very attractive man. He's in his uniform, which isn't a surprise because he and Charlie are on similar schedules despite working different beats.

It *is* a surprise that he doesn't smile back. I feel my face fall.

Josh cocks his head in the direction he's just come from. "Can you join me in Ted's office, Ash?"

There's something off about his tone. He's too calm. Too measured. I don't like it at all.

I swallow and nod, ignoring the stares of my colleagues around me. He puts his hand on my back as we walk down the hall to Ted's private office, a huge room with floor-to-ceiling windows that look out over the city toward the mountains.

When we get there, Ted's leaning against the window looking pensive. His hair's messed up, like he's been running his hands through it. His face is tense. His strong jaw is clenched, and stress lines pull his forehead down. Josh shuts the door behind me, and I look between both men, getting the distinct impression that they've already spoken.

This is confirmed by the silent conversation they seem to have, before Ted pushes off from the window and moves around his desk, leaning against the side of the glass and chrome monstrosity which is home to his laptop and not much else. Without speaking, Josh guides me into the seat right in front of Ted and then crouches at my side.

Red flags abound. My chest tightens.

"What's going on?" I ask, but my gut knows it's not going to be good news.

Josh swallows, and I'm finally noticing just how pale and shaken he looks. "There's been an…incident."

My heart speeds up and I put two and two together. "Where's Charlie?"

Josh's expression shutters and I *know*. It's bad news. It's bad news, and it's about Charlie.

"Josh…" My mouth is dry, and I can barely get the question out. "What happened? *Where's Charlie?*" This time I sound more demanding. Panicked, even.

While Josh starts to explain that Charlie and Max were responding to a call, I'm barely aware of Ted moving closer to me. When Josh tells me that Charlie was shot —*twice*— in a case of bad timing, I feel like I'm having an out of body experience.

"No…" I say and shake my head, refusing to believe the man in front of me. "No, it wasn't Charlie. I saw Charlie this morning. He… he…" He'd given me a very quick blow job because he was still riding the high from the weekend, still calling me his big, brave boy and thanking me for being everything he's ever wanted in a Little and a lover. For trusting him.

After returning the favor, I'd snuggled back into the pillows and gone back to sleep as he left for the early shift. I hadn't even told him that I loved him.

"He's in surgery," Josh says. He squeezes my thigh in what I assume is meant to be a reassuring gesture. "Mom and Dad are there. So are Maisy and Axel."

I haven't met any of Charlie's family yet. Not outside of Josh. Is that weird? We've been together for over six months now, and I've only met his friends from the kink community.

Oh, God, did he never want me to meet them? Has he even told them about me?

That makes my chest squeeze harder.

Am I that embarrassing?

Does he not feel the same way about this relationship as I do?

Because even if the world finds out that I'm his boy and he's my Daddy, as long as I have him it's okay. It's okay because he's worth the uncomfortable conversations. He's worth the momentary sting of judgment from people who don't get it but whose opinions ultimately don't matter. He's worth everything to me.

"I... Did you want me to stay away?" My voice breaks as I ask the question, but if Charlie hasn't told his family about me, it would make sense not to be there.

"What?" Josh frowns, and he almost sounds insulted. He pushes back to his feet, staring down at me incredulously. "Why?"

I want to try and explain the jumble of concerns in my head, but the tears are starting to flow. I'm scared for Charlie, and confused about his family, and can feel the anxiety building as my chest squeezes.

"Okay, kiddo, breathe," Ted says soothingly, pulling me up from the chair and into his hug. He's not Charlie, but I've spent enough time with him now that I'm comfortable with him when Daddy can't be there. Over the top of my head, he asks Josh, "Has Ash met any of your family?"

I sniffle and answer before Josh can. "No."

Josh groans. "And you think, what? You're Charlie's dirty little secret?" He sounds derisive and mean, like I'm an idiot for jumping to that conclusion.

I flinch.

"*Josh*," Ted snaps, and I press my face into his shoulder while I try to get my tears back under control. "I know you're stressed, but don't take it out on Ash."

There's a moment of silence before Josh sighs. "Sorry. I'm just…" He makes a frustrated sound. "Ash, Charlie loves you. *Of course* he's told Mom and Dad about you. And Maisy and Axel, too. But…our family is *a lot*, and he wanted to make sure you were comfortable before he unleashed them all on you." Then he chuckles a little. "I'm honestly surprised Mom hasn't just turned up on your doorstep yet."

"Really?" I look up and turn to face him, wanting to be sure he's not just giving me lip service.

He nods. "And, look, they don't know about the whole Daddy/boy BDSM thing, but that's partially because Charlie's never had anyone he's been serious enough with to explain it to them. Neither have I, for that matter."

"Oh." I think that through for a moment. It's not surprising. Not many people would want their parents knowing about their sex lives, vanilla or otherwise. "That's understandable," I finally respond. "I can stay Big. That's easy to do, especially around strangers."

Josh cocks an eyebrow at me. "How'd we meet again?"

I can't help snorting. "Those were extenuating circumstances."

"Yeah." His face falls, the amusement fading as quickly as it appeared. "But so are these."

He's got a point. Can I hold it together and not drop into Little space in front of his parents?

"It's not going to matter if you slip," he tells me, as though he's read my mind. "Charlie loves you and they're gonna love you."

Swallowing, I can only nod because I don't want to argue with him about my fears. Not when the bigger issue is whether the man I love is going to be okay or not. Suddenly, with that thought, I can't be here any longer. I need to be where Charlie is, even if he's not conscious. "Can we go to the hospital?"

When Josh nods, I turn back to Ted. I've never taken him up on his offer to stand in for Charlie when he's not able to be there for me —not without Charlie arranging it himself— but I don't think I can do this alone. "Will you come, too?"

Ted has babysat me, for lack of a better term, on evenings when Charlie's worked late, and he's been around the house a lot. Daddy's been trying to coax me into calling the other man Uncle Ted, but in the office that just feels weird. Still, if there's anyone I can rely on to be a caregiver in Charlie's absence, it's Ted, and I know Charlie trusts him, too. The fact that I know this makes it easier. There's no sexual or romantic aspect in our interactions, just pure comfort, and I need that now more than ever.

"I wouldn't be anywhere else, little one," he tells me, kissing the top of my head. "It's going to be okay."

"You can't promise that."

"For my sake," he confesses, and I feel selfish because he cares about Charlie, too. "I have to believe it."

* * *

At the hospital, Josh's uniformed presence helps get us moved straight back into the private waiting room for families awaiting news of ER patients. He strides in first and I watch as he's swarmed by the other four people already in the room, enveloped into an emotional group hug.

There's an older man who looks so much like him and Charlie that it takes my breath away, and a short, curvy woman with riotous, dark, curly hair who must be their mom. The younger woman's hair is straight and platinum blonde. She's a bit shorter than Josh and reed thin. I assume she's Maisy. She doesn't look much older than Josh, and she has the same nose as her brothers and shares the same blue eyes as Charlie and their dad. Then there's the younger guy, who must be Axel. He looks more like their mother than the others, shorter and stockier, his hair curly like hers.

I stand back, pressed up against Ted, my insecurities getting the better of me until Josh and Charlie's mom looks over and gasps.

"You must be Ash," she declares, already pulling away from the group to tug me into a hug. The top of her head barely reaches my shoulder. She's soft and warm and her hug makes my breathing hitch. My mom died when I was four, so I don't really remember this sort of maternal affection, but I love it.

"Oh, sweetheart." She reaches up and brushes back my curls which are getting a bit long. "I'm sorry we had to meet this way. You're just the sweetest thing, aren't you?"

"Mom," Josh says with a warning in his tone; but she waves him off, takes me by the hand and tugs me toward the rest of the family. Over her shoulder, she glances back at Ted. "Come on, Theodore; you too."

I want to laugh, because it's not often I see Ted get bossed around by anyone, let alone a short, matronly woman.

"I'm Marie," she introduces herself, then points to her husband, "and this is Grant. These are Charlie's sister and brother, Maisy and Axel. I've heard you know Josh."

I nod at everyone in turn. "Yes, ma'am."

"None of that. It's Marie or Mom," she insists, and I can definitely see where Charlie gets his take-charge, hold-no-prisoners attitude from. The same one that saw him inviting me to live with him almost instantly. I think I love this woman already for that reason alone.

"Okay," I answer, not using either name because I'm not ready yet.

"Let the poor boy breathe, Marie," Grant chides, but his tone is full of affection. Everything about this family radiates support and warmth, and it settles my nerves about meeting them.

There's a knock at the door, and we turn as a group to see a blond cop hovering at the threshold, his uniform stained and rumpled. Josh stomps over to him and wraps his arms around him. I blink. I don't hear the murmured words they exchange, but there's a lot of manly back thumping as they part.

Josh gestures between the group and the other cop. "Everyone, Max Dalton. Max, everyone."

Max. Charlie's partner. My gaze zeroes in on the stains on his shirt and pants. That's Charlie's blood, I'm betting. I feel woozy.

"Down he goes," Ted says, catching me as my knees buckle.

"Sorry." I feel my cheeks burn as he eases me into a chair. I can feel everyone's gazes on me. "I just…blood…" I swallow back bile.

"Shit," Max curses, looking down at himself. He looks over at me, genuinely apologetic. "I didn't think. The paramedics let me go; I had to give my statement and then I came straight here." He looks across to Josh. "Any update?"

Josh shakes his head. "Not yet. I only just got here."

Max sinks into a chair by the door. And then we all wait. Marie peppers me with questions, and I can tell it's partially to distract us from the not-knowing, but also because she really is excited to meet me, even if the circumstances aren't ideal. They're not difficult questions —stuff like where I grew up, my favorite foods, whether I enjoy my job— and they help keep me from breaking down. When a doctor enters the room, though, we all fall silent.

"You're here for Charlie Walker?" the man asks, taking in the assembled group. We all nod.

"Okay, he's out of surgery, it went well" —there's a collective sigh of relief, and Marie and I both sob a little, clutching each other's hands— "and he's awake, but heavily medicated." He looks over us all and frowns. "I'm afraid we can only let two visitors in for now, and he'll need rest."

"You go," I tell his mother. "I'll come back tomorrow."

"That's not happening," Josh argues, shaking his head. "I know Charlie. He'll ask for you, Ash."

I want that. I desperately do. But it doesn't feel right. "Over his own parents? I can't…"

"You and Marie both go," Grant says in a tone that brooks

no arguments. *Huh. Maybe Charlie gets a little of his Daddy vibe from him, after all.* "Then we'll all come back tomorrow and take shifts."

Have I mentioned that I love his parents?

Chapter Sixteen — Charlie

The antiseptic smell of the hospital hits me before I open my eyes. I wince against the bright lights and groan, disoriented. A doctor checks my vision briefly, asks me what I remember —getting out of the car, gunfire, yelling— and nods, explaining that I took two bullets. It feels surreal. I'm not the kind of cop that gets shot at. I'm not a detective. I don't even usually work Robbery and Homicide. My life isn't like an episode of *Law & Order*.

"You were lucky," the surgeon tells me. "The bullet in your thigh missed the femoral artery by a fraction of an inch. We were able to successfully remove the bullet intact. You suffered a femur fracture, though, for which we needed to insert a metal rod into the bone. You're going to need crutches for a while and a physical therapy regimen to regain full movement. Recovery's probably going to take a few months." He tilts his head to the side. "The second was to your right pectoral and was a clean shot through. No significant damage, but you'll have some scar tissue on your chest and shoulder blade. I expect you'll probably need physical therapy to prevent muscular atrophy in your chest and shoulder, too."

I nod as I take this in, my brain still fuzzy.

"Are you in any pain?"

I have a dull ache in my chest and my thigh, but other than that, I can't feel anything. I shake my head. "No." My mouth is dry and feels like it's been stuffed with cotton balls. I try to clear my throat, which hurts. I assume they put a tube down it during surgery. "Water?"

A nurse materializes from out of nowhere and hands me a cup with a straw. "Sip it to start," she instructs, and it's difficult not to slurp it all down, but I do as I'm told.

"They've got you on the good stuff, so I'm not surprised nothing hurts." The doctor carries on with an amused little smile. "And I wouldn't be surprised if you're still sleepy. You're going to need to rest for a bit." He pauses. "You've got quite the number of visitors out there. We can only send two people in, but I'll let them all know you're going to pull through."

I frown, the words taking a while to process. By the time I move to ask about Ash —who is probably going out of his mind with worry— the doctor's already gone.

I try to stay awake, but my eyes are heavy, and I doze off before the doctor comes back.

* * *

When I wake up again, I can feel the pain. My leg and chest hurt like a bitch. I groan, once again disoriented, and I blink as I get used to the light again.

"Charlie." My mother's voice, full of relief and love, makes me wince. I've got a headache, too, apparently. "Oh, sweetheart, you're awake."

"Mom," I moan. "Volume down. Jesus."

There's a gentle, tinkling —but still watery— giggle from the other side of the bed and I whip my head over, suddenly unconcerned with how bright everything is. I still squint, though. "Ash?"

He leans forward and grasps my hand, careful of the IV line attached to the back of it. "You scared me, Charlie," he murmurs, pressing a kiss to the inside of my palm. His soft lips against my skin are a healing balm for my soul.

"I'm so sorry, baby." What else can I say? Even though none of this was my fault, I left him alone and worried.

He smiles softly at me, then glances over my head. "So…I met your mom…"

"Yeah; I apologize for anything she's said or done while I've been out of it."

She smacks my uninjured left shoulder lightly. "Behave, Charles."

I make a face. "Ugh. Really? I almost *died*, Mom, you can let up with the 'Charles' crap." Even though it was meant to be a joke, I watch my mother's eyes fill with tears and hear the shaky inhalation from my boyfriend and… Alright, I'll admit it, my comedic timing sucks right now. Blame the morphine. "Shit. Sorry. I was trying to lighten the mood."

"You're an idiot," Ash observes.

I turn my head to face him and look him over properly. His eyes are red rimmed but sharp. There's no sense of Little Ash about him. I'm surprised that he's not even hovering near the brink of his Little headspace. I'm glad, but surprised.

"Ted talked me down from my anxiety attack," Ash offers, as though he can read my thoughts on my face. "And your family

138

is amazing, too. I'm gonna keep your mom if it's all the same to you."

Above me to my left, my mother laughs and pats my shoulder. It's her sign that she's happy for me and that she approves of my boyfriend. A little "don't fuck this up" and a lot "we're keeping him, too." I blink back tears.

God, I love this man. He's worked through his issues with his boss seeing him Little because he knows how much Ted's friendship means to me. And his easy acceptance of my intense (but admittedly loving) family brings a lump of pure emotion to my throat.

I already knew that I loved him, but this...this is unlike anything I've ever felt before. It's an all-encompassing, soul-wrenching, gut-clenching feeling that lifts me up and terrifies me in equal measures. If I were to lose him now, it would destroy me.

Clearing my throat, I squeeze his fingers back. "I love you, Ash. So much."

His expression says it all, his eyes shining the way I know mine are, his full lips turned upward into a soft, emotional smile. He gets up and leans over me, still holding my hand, to bring our lips together. But, before they meet, he pauses. I can feel his breath on my lips. "I love you too, Charlie." Then he kisses me so carefully —soft, chaste, and sweet— and it's not enough. Not nearly enough. But it's also everything.

* * *

I'm moved into a private room the next day, and when visiting hours open, it feels like everyone I've ever met pours in through the doors. Naturally, my family and closest friends arrive first.

Then Max, who is tearing himself up over the whole incident, even though neither of us had anticipated the events as they unfolded.

I do know that if he hadn't acted so quickly, compressing the blood flow and calling in the shooting, I would have bled out, so I tell him as much. I've never seen my partner as anything other than stoic or jovial, and it rattles me to see him this way. Josh steps in and repeats everything I've said, adding details that have made their way around the precinct in the hours since it all went down. Nobody blames Max, and we both did everything by the book.

Max has been put on desk duty, though, and needs a psych clearance before he can return to the beat. That's hardly a surprise to any of us —it's standard practice— but I can tell it's grating on him.

Then some of the other guys from the station come in, wanting to see for themselves that I'm alive, and things turn somber when my Captain joins us. I'm aware that my leg injury puts my future in the force on the line, but when he says it out loud, it's like I'm losing a part of me. With the metal rod in my leg, it's not likely I'll get medical clearance to return, even if I do get a full range of motion back; but he doesn't know for sure, and we all pretend to be hopeful.

I start making backup plans anyway.

At some point the stream of visitors abates, and I'm left alone with Ash for the first time in far too long. I shuffle toward the right side of my bed —my injured side— and pat the space I've opened on the left. "C'mere, little lamb."

Cautiously, he snuggles into my side, and we both sigh in contentment. In addition to my concerns about my career, I'm worried that my injuries are going to make it difficult for me to be the Daddy he needs. Sex is probably going to be off the table while my leg recovers, but it's the other stuff —crawling around on the floor with him during playtime, kneeling beside the tub for bath time, sitting him in my lap, lifting and carrying him— that I'm really concerned about. The next few months are going to suck, and I don't want to disappoint him.

I keep these thoughts to myself, though. Once I've spoken to the physical therapist, I'll know what I'm really working with. Until then, we're just going to have to get creative.

"I really do love your family," Ash says, breaking the silence that's descended between us. He nuzzles his head into the hollow of my throat and my arm tightens around him. "They are…" He pauses and weighs his words. "…boisterous, but they've been so sweet to include me in everything."

Josh has already told me that my family dragged Ash and Ted along with them to dinner last night, and that Maisy's been doing her best to keep Mom from smothering him with too much affection. Not that I think there is such a thing as too much affection when it comes to my boy. He soaks it up like a sponge, and I'm starting to guess that he never had enough of it growing up.

"Even Axel's showing his inner Daddy around him," Josh had teased.

I can see that being a thing. Ash has this air about him —even when he's Big— that seems to beg for love and protection. Considering those big, hazel eyes, the soft curls on his head, and his youthful face, it's hard not to want to wrap him in bubble wrap and keep him safe.

"Let me know if they get to be too much," I tell Ash as I pull myself out of my thoughts. "It happens. They drive me crazy and I'm used to them."

"I mean… Your mom asked me what size underwear I wear, so…I can see that."

I groan and close my eyes. "*Mom…*"

Ash giggles and attempts to snuggle closer. Unless he can somehow melt into me via osmosis, he's already as close as he can get. But the feel of him, warm and solid against me, is everything I need right now. "She means well. I think she wanted to bring me a change of clothes because I don't want to go home."

My heart sinks. "Baby, you're going to have to go eventually."

I feel him go tense. "I don't want to." I can't see his face, but I can hear him pouting. It's the first sign of Little Ash I've seen since I woke up here.

"Asher…"

"No."

I pause. I'm not exactly sure how to proceed here. He's pushing boundaries, but at the same time he's likely reacting to the fear and stress of yesterday's events. It's not fair to discipline him for that; however, the way he's channeling those feelings isn't appropriate. "Ash."

He shakes his head, pressing his face harder into me. His shoulders shake under my arm, and yeah, there's no way I'm going to get stern with him.

"Baby, I'm okay…" I say as the first tears hit the skin of my neck.

"I was so scared," he cries, and it breaks my heart all over again.

"I know."

"I thought I was going to lose you."

"I know."

"I don't know what I'd do if—"

142

"Ash, don't. I'm okay. I'm going to be back home before you know it." I'm not playing the game of what-ifs. I refuse.

He sniffles and I rub his back. "I need you, Daddy."

A tear escapes from the corner of my eye and runs down my cheek. My throat is clogged with emotion, and I can't promise him that I'll be the man he needs me to be. Not for a few months, maybe not ever again, depending on the damage to my leg. But I swallow over the lump and try to ignore those doubts. "You've got me, little lamb," I tell him, my voice tight and gruff. "You've got me."

He dozes off against me, and this is how Ted finds us an hour or so later. He knocks on the open door of my room and smiles indulgently at the scene he walks in on.

"I need you to look after him." The plea falls from my lips before Ted makes it even halfway across the room. "I don't know how long I'll be here, and he can't stay forever, and—"

"You don't even need to ask," Ted assures me, sitting in the seat to my right. The seat Ash has been using for the most part. He leans forward, narrowing his brown eyes, assessing me. "How are you doing? And I mean really, Charlie."

Double-checking that Ash is asleep, measuring the slow, even puffs of breath that coast over my chest, I sigh. "I don't know." I'm not used to admitting weakness or exposing my own vulnerability. But Ted's the big brother I never had, and I need his guidance as much as I did when I first met him.

He arches an eyebrow, and my worries all spill out. I tell him about the likely end of my career, of not knowing what the hell I'm going to do if that happens. I describe the few backup plans I've had that sound crazy to even my own ears and are probably morphine-induced ravings. Then I move on to my worries about how I'm going to be the person —the Daddy—

Ash needs me to be while I'm physically unable to do the things we enjoy.

By the time I've vented all of my worries, I feel lighter for having shared them, but guilty for not having shared them with Ash. So then, on a whisper, I confess that to Ted as well.

He takes it all in, nodding and asking questions quietly as I ramble, then sits back and shakes his head at me when I'm done.

"Do you honestly think he's going to care that you can't crawl around on the floor with him?" he asks, bypassing my worries about my career entirely. I'm honestly glad that he does, because I think we both know that those are surface concerns at best. "Or that you'll probably be limited to blow jobs and hand jobs for a bit?" Ted cocks his head, giving me his best are-you-completely-stupid look. "If the tables were turned, would you care if he couldn't?"

"No," I answer without hesitation. I close my eyes and take a deep breath. "But...I'm supposed to—"

"I'm an adult." Ash's voice interrupts me, and I wonder just how long he's been awake. He sits up and gives me the exact same look Ted just did. "We're equals in this, Charlie. It's a give and take. And just because you're dominant doesn't mean you can't be vulnerable and need help sometimes. Just like my being submissive doesn't mean I'm weak and helpless."

I scramble to fix the mess I've just made. "I never said—"

"I know." His voice turns soft, and I relax because he's not angry with me or hurt by my assumptions. "But, Charlie, I don't love you *just* because you play with me, or because you're big and strong, or even because we're great in bed together. I love you for this." He splays his hand over my heart, which attempts to beat its way out of my chest when he touches it.

144

The increased beeping on the monitor beside me gives me away and I blush. Ash continues sagely, "And I love you for the person you are inside. The rest is fun, but we can work around it. We can get creative."

The unknowing way he echoes my original attempt to console myself makes me smile. "Yeah?" I ask him, waggling my eyebrows suggestively.

He chuckles. "Yeah."

My tone dips low and flirtatious, and I'm already forgetting my worries. "I'd like to know what sort of creative ideas you have."

"I'm still in the room," Ted says through some obviously fake coughing, and the moment between me and Ash is broken, though we laugh about it.

Despite the lighter mood, I'm still concerned about Ash being alone at home while I'm stuck in a hospital bed. Bracing myself, I squeeze his hip and say, "You still need your Little time while I'm here, baby. And I know you don't enjoy it on your own."

I don't tell him that I know he can function without it, because I don't want him to have to try. It helps him manage his stress levels, and I can't help but think that he'll be even more stressed while I'm recovering from being shot. But I don't say any of this because he knows it already.

Instead of fighting me, he sighs. "What do you suggest?"

Chapter Seventeen — Asher

"I'll swing by my place, grab some stuff, and come back here if you're good with that," Ted says as he pulls his car up at home.

Charlie convinced me to come back here while conceding that there's nothing stopping me from visiting him every day. Well, nothing except for work, but seeing as my boss is now also my live-in babysitter, I feel like it's not going to be an issue.

Ted's going to be staying in the adult guest room for the next few nights. Just until Charlie's released from the hospital. We talked the whole plan through.

As much as I hate being away from Charlie, I know he's right. My Little time, even if it's only an hour or so a day, helps ground me. In addition to that, I'm most comfortable being Little at home, usually with a playmate or with my Daddy at my side. Without either of those things, Ted's not a bad stand-in. I'm used to his presence, and he's not bad at coloring or playing race cars with me. He's not a huge fan of teddy bear tea parties, but I'm working on changing that. His next Little will thank me.

When I'm with Ted, I don't go too deep into Little space. I don't want help changing or bathing, and I don't use —or even wear— diapers. I go just far enough to relax and enjoy playtime and story time, and I still like having a bottle and being cuddled to sleep. I've also told Ted that I don't feel right being put to bed in the primary suite without Charlie there, so I'll be crashing in my kid's room for the time being.

Realizing that Ted is waiting for an answer, I nod. "Sorry, my mind was elsewhere."

He gives me a sad little smile and leans over to rub my shoulder. "It's okay, Ash. It's been a rough couple of days."

He sounds just as wrung out as I feel. Guilt lances through me. "You don't have to stay here," I rush to tell him. "Your job is stressful and busy enough as it is without having to be Uncle Ted." I offer him a rueful smile. "Charlie worries about me, but I *can* function on my own."

"Nobody's questioning that," he assures me seriously. "But someone you love is in the hospital, and being alone through that…" Ted gets a distant look in his eye. "Well, it sucks." Giving himself a little shake, he pins his best Uncle Ted stare on me again. "I want to be here. To be honest, I think it's as much for me as it is for you."

I don't question him. His best friend just got shot. If he says he needs company, I'm going to have to take his words at face value. "Okay," I answer softly. "Go get your stuff and I'll organize something for dinner." I don't tell him that if he weren't staying over, I would just have a bowl of cereal.

Looking left to right, Ted leans in again with a playful little grin. "*Or* we can get takeout and not tell your Daddy?"

For the first time in over twenty-four hours, I feel a spark of childish glee. With my eyes going wide and a genuine smile stretching across my face, I clap my hands. "This is why you're my favorite Uncle Ted."

"Hey! I'm your *only* Uncle Ted!" He darts out a hand and tickles me, and I squirm and squeal and leave the car feeling lighter than I imagined I could when I left the hospital earlier.

* * *

Ted drops me off at the hospital every morning on his way to work. He's arranged for me to have time off until Charlie's released —which should be in a couple more days— and I have to admit that having him staying with me has helped keep my mind off the fact that Charlie could have died.

Not that Ted's presence has helped keep the nightmares at bay, but he has cuddled with me on the couch, watching cartoons in the middle of the night, and he's carried me back to my bed when I've drifted off to sleep against him. He's been kind enough not to mention the nightmares after the fact, but I know he's itching for me to talk the issue through with him. I don't plan on doing that, but it's a comfort to know he's here for me.

Today's the fourth day of this new routine, and when I walk into Charlie's hospital room, his nurse is removing the IV line from his hand.

"Look, babe." He beams at me, his beard now reminding me of all my dirty lumberjack fantasies because he hasn't been able to trim it. "I'm losing the cords. One step closer to freedom."

His color is looking better, and his eyes have lost that drugged-up, glazed look. "They've taken you off the meds, huh?"

"Finally," Charlie says with a bob of his head. It's good to see him like this. For the past couple of days, he's been on edge and snappish, feeling trapped and useless and fidgety. We haven't fought, but our easy camaraderie hasn't been there either. "Tylenol only from here on out."

There's a part of me that wonders if that's going to be enough, but I know better than to question it out loud. Charlie's desperate to come home, and I'm not going to say anything that might suggest I don't think he's ready, even though I don't know how he'll manage getting up and down the stairs.

"No more monitors either?" I ask, watching as the nurse starts wheeling the equipment aside, having already removed the sensors that were taped to his chest and clipped to his finger. To my eyes, he immediately looks healthier without anything attached to him.

"Nope." Charlie's blue eyes glitter as the nurse leaves the room. "*And* I'll be able to take a piss by myself."

I can't help snorting. He's hated that he's had to rely on someone to come and help him drag his IV line and monitors everywhere while also using crutches because he can't put any weight on his right leg. To tease him, I lower my voice and say, "Sometimes having Daddy help is fun."

With fire in his eyes, Charlie groans. "Fuck, I miss you." His hand, now blessedly free of wires and tubes, goes to his crotch and he squeezes himself through the thin hospital blanket.

"*Charlie.*" I shake my head, laughter bubbling up while I try to sound scandalized. "You're in a hospital bed."

A bit of unease sets in when he continues to fondle himself shamelessly.

Oblivious, he waggles his dark eyebrows at me. "So? We could play doctor."

My dick is on board. I am not. "I'm not into exhibitionism," I remind him. It was something we discussed when we went over our hard limits. The idea of someone walking in and catching us spikes my anxiety.

I don't even like secondhand embarrassment when I'm watching a movie.

The unease turns to something darker, tendrils of panic beginning to unfurl in my belly, but Charlie's still playful, unaware of the turn my thoughts are taking. "You can just watch me then."

My gaze flits to the open door, my heart hammering. No longer feeling amused at all, I shake my head. I *can't.*

Memories of being caught kissing my first boyfriend by my father —*just kissing*— have my palms sweaty and nausea churning in my gut.

I know this isn't the same thing, but the feelings are similar and there's no thrill in potentially being caught. Not for me. "Red light, Charlie."

He stops immediately, all merriment ceasing. I immediately feel guilty. I assume the feeling is written all over my face and I look to the ground, scuffing my worn sneaker over the linoleum.

"Ash, baby," Charlie reaches for me, tugging me onto the bed at his side and I go willingly, needing the comfort. "I'm proud of you for safe wording."

"It's so stupid," I mutter. "You were being sexy. It wasn't even *me* who would have been caught doing something naughty." But I would have been a party to it. My stomach is still churning with discomfort.

"You were uncomfortable and I pushed the envelope. I'm sorry."

He's full of remorse and I hate that, too.

"This is why safe words exist," I say as I relax into his side. "You were being playful, and it's not like you were asking me to get naked or fuck you or anything. But…the whole idea of getting caught doing anything sexual… It's a trigger for me." And not one we've had any reason to discuss. Well, not until now. But instead of explaining why, I acknowledge, "I safe worded and you stopped straight away. That means everything to me, Charlie."

"Nobody in the lifestyle worth their salt wouldn't," he refutes gently, and I nod. But he continues, "And never *ever* feel guilty for safe wording. Never. It's not a weakness. The whole point of the games we play is that we enjoy ourselves. If one of us isn't into it —*especially* if it's making one of us uncomfortable— stopping is the *only* option."

"Okay," I answer quietly.

After another moment, Charlie cuddles me a little bit tighter and kisses the top of my head. "You don't need to explain why you safe worded, either. I mean, as your boyfriend and Daddy, I want to know so I don't accidentally trigger you in other ways, but it's your prerogative whether you want to tell me or not." His hand shifts from my side, sliding up over my bicep and into my hair. "But I know now that public displays of indecency for either of us are definitely a no-go."

"Yeah… I didn't think it would make me feel like it did, to be honest," I tell him with a shrug. "I just… It reminded me of the way I accidentally outed myself to my dad."

Charlie stiffens. Considering he knows that the man kicked me out of home for buying myself diapers, he knows the story doesn't end well.

I pick at a loose threat in the blanket on Charlie's stomach. "I was sixteen. He used to work late, so I invited Jack —my first boyfriend— over. We were making out on the couch, and I didn't hear Dad's truck pull into the driveway."

Even now, my heart thuds painfully with the memory of the door opening, of the screaming, of the way he threatened Jack and the fact that Jack never even looked at me again after that. The names Dad called me. The slap to my face. The threats of what would happen if he ever caught me with a boy again.

Haltingly, I tell Charlie all of it. I'm shaking a little by the end, but I haven't cried. I refuse to ever cry over my father again.

"Jesus." Charlie exhales the word, holding me tight. Instead of reiterating his thoughts that my father is an asshole —which I know he thinks, and I wholeheartedly agree with him— he gives me exactly what I need. He lightens the mood. "And here I thought having my mom sit me and my first boyfriend down at the kitchen table, handing us condoms and lube and talking about the best positions for first-time anal penetration was traumatizing."

Laughter bursts out of me, and I'm cackling so hard I can barely breathe. As I finally calm down, wiping tears from my eyes, I manage, "I want to say 'She didn't?!' but having met your mom… Yeah, I can totally imagine that."

"Oh, she did. But it was better than the time she sat Maisy down to watch a birthing video." Charlie shudders. "*Maisy's* birth, at that."

"Oh my God. *Why?*"

"Let's just say Mom's brand of sexual education is… disturbing at best. Pretty sure Maisy abstained until college. Honestly, I can acknowledge that Mom pushes things too far sometimes. She means well, and I love her, but I can admit that it's not okay to do the things she does."

"She's still a good person, and I like her." Snuggling against him and determined to get him to smile again, I follow my assessment with a demand to hear more of the ludicrous stories from his youth, and he indulges me like a good Daddy should.

Chapter Eighteen — Charlie

I shouldn't be surprised to find a billion people at home when I'm finally released from my sterile prison. Ted drove, because with my right leg out of action I can't drive without clearance from my physical therapist. I sat in the back seat with Ash, who is being a real mother hen. I want to ask him which of us is the Daddy, but I'm letting him have this for now because I get it. He almost lost me. I suspect that when he's Little for me, he's going to be clingy as fuck...and damn if that doesn't warm and excite me in all the possible ways. I love it when he's needy. It's a thrill to feel wanted by my boy.

I hobble up the front steps, relying on the handrail while Ash shoulders my bulk on the other side with his arm wrapped securely around my waist. I can already hear the cacophony of voices from inside. If the cars lining my usually quiet suburban street hadn't been a dead giveaway, the commotion is.

"Did you invite the entire city?" I ask Ash when we reach the top of the front steps and he hands me my crutches.

"Nah," he says. "Only, like, a quarter of it."

I'm getting better with the crutches, I have to admit. Putting my weight on my left leg and swinging forward with my right, I make my way through the doorway and down the short hall from the little foyer. My family's in the living area, and with a start I realize Ash's toys are neatly tucked into the corner next to the couch, on display for everyone to see. Hell, Josh is even sitting on the end of the couch, absentmindedly rolling one of Ash's toy cars over his thigh. There's no excuse for the toys' existence —I don't have any nieces or nephews, and my friends don't have kids— and I look back at Ash, gauging his reaction.

I'm surprised when he doesn't even blink at the concept of our secret lives being outed. Or maybe he hasn't made that connection yet?

At my arched eyebrow, he moves in close and says, "Your mom worked it out. She and your dad turned up here one night with a casserole..." He shrugs, like it's no big deal. "I was in my pj's and playing with my water mat, and Ted couldn't exactly turn them away."

I'm going to get the whole story out of him later, but he doesn't seem panicked or upset, so I'm going to just go with it. "Okay..."

"Ted kind of gave them the CliffsNotes version. They, uh, they know he's also part of the lifestyle..." His cheeks burn. "Having to explain that, no, I'm not sleeping with you *and* Ted was awkward."

I laugh at that, and the sound catches my parents' attention. Mom's off the couch like lightning, rushing forward and wrapping her arms around my middle like a short, plump linebacker going in for a tackle.

"Mom," I complain as she almost knocks me off balance, "it's almost as if you don't know I'm injured."

There's zero remorse from my mother. Instead, she says, "You're a big boy, Daddy, and you can take a hug from your mother."

"Please don't call me Daddy ever again." I cringe. "That's so wrong coming from you."

At the same time, her easy acceptance of my lifestyle choice feels good. She ushers me into my own living room and pushes me to sit on the couch. "I've been reading a lot about BDSM since Theodore explained the situation."

Flashbacks to her lectures on gay sex have me already struggling to get back to my feet so I can escape. My cheeks are on fire. "Mom. Stop." I look to Ash, who is covering his mouth with his hand, trying to stifle his amusement. *Traitor*. "Ash, help."

Mom shakes her head. "Oh, no, I think he needs to hear this, too…"

"Actually, sorry, I can hear Spencer calling for help with the grill," he says, flouncing out of the room.

That brat is getting the spanking of a lifetime for this. Or an hour in the corner.

Turning to my father, who looks mildly uncomfortable, I beg, "Come on, Dad. Stop her. This is madness."

"I've tried." He follows his words with the same beleaguered sigh that he gives every time she does something like this. "It's not like I want to hear about your sex life, either."

"I'm thirty-one! *Nobody* in this room needs to be talking about my sex life."

This. *This* is why I wanted to keep my family and Ash separate.

Josh snorts from the end of the couch, and I cast him a filthy look. If I weren't such a good brother, I'd consider outing him, too. But that is an epic douche move, and I wouldn't forgive myself if I did it, tempting as it is to turn my mother's "research" on him.

"I'll be honest, I'm going to second that," Chance says, leaning against the archway between the dining area and the living room. He lifts his bearded chin at me. "I've been sent to come resc—er...get you."

"Nice save," I respond dryly. "Very smooth."

He crosses the room and extends a hand, helping me to my feet and keeping me steady until I can get my crutches under my arms again. We make our way out through the dining area and kitchen to the deck out back. Not wanting to be left out, my family trails behind us.

The rest of the gang is here, and I'm not surprised to find Max at the table as well. Ash is leaning against the wall near the grill, chatting with Spencer, who is flipping burgers. When Ash sees me, he pulls the nearest chair out and gestures for me to sit, giving me a quick peck on the lips before leaning against the side of the chair. I want nothing more than to pull him into my lap, but with the wound from my surgery still pretty fresh, I can't.

Spence offers me a sympathetic grimace. "How long 'til the stitches come out?" he asks, guessing my predicament correctly.

"Not soon enough," I grumble.

Ash's hand runs through my hair in a soothing gesture. "We'll get through it, Daddy."

With how sweet and optimistic he sounds, I can't help but believe it.

* * *

Ash's cries wake me up in the middle of the night. I shoot up into a seated position against the headboard, regretting the rapid movement instantly. Pain radiates from my shoulder and thigh, and I grit my teeth.

Ted told me that Ash has been having nightmares, but a part of me had hoped that my being home again might relieve some of his anxiety. However, even though we're in the same bed, we're not spooned up together as we normally would be. I have to sleep on my back while I heal, and Ash is terrified of jostling and hurting me. So, instead of being pressed up against my side, he's curled in a fetal position on the far edge of the mattress. It's a king-size bed, and the distance between us makes my heart sink.

"Baby." I reach for him, rolling onto my uninjured side, my fingers skimming his tense shoulders. "Wake up. It's just a bad dream."

Ash comes to slowly, then turns to face me. I catch the sheen of tears on his cheeks, lit by the sliver of moonlight filtering in through the gap in the curtains. The guilt on his face breaks my heart, though.

"Sorry," he whispers into the silence. "I didn't mean to wake you."

He's never apologized for the nightmares. Not even on that first night when we were relative strangers. I can't explain why this hurts me so much to hear now, but it makes me ache inside. Swallowing roughly, I extend my arm. "Come here, little lamb."

He hesitates and it twists the knife a little further.

"Asher." He never fails to respond to my firm tone, but tonight it feels wrong to use it like this. "Come here."

As he finally rolls into my embrace, his head comes to rest on my shoulder. He's not crying, but I can feel his shoulders trembling. Running my hand through his soft curls, I try to soothe us both. "Are we going to talk about it?"

He shakes his head.

In those early days of our relationship, I never pushed. But this feels bigger somehow. He apologized for no reason. I hate that. Earlier today, I thought that we'd be able to get through this, but maybe it's not the case.

I hate that my being injured has put limitations on our relationship. I hate that he no longer feels like he can wake me up when he has a bad dream. I hate that my fears of not being able to be the Daddy he needs appear to be coming true.

No. No, I refuse to accept that. I need to grow up and force the issue, even if it means I'm the one who has to be vulnerable first right now.

With a shaky inhale, I start talking. "I can't lose you, Ash. I know that things are going to suck for a while, that I can't do all the Daddy things—"

His body stiffens and he sounds horrified. "What? No, I don't care about—"

"I know," I assure him, "but...you had a nightmare, baby. And you pulled away instead of coming to me and..." My voice cracks and Ash's hold on me tightens. After a moment, when I feel calm enough, I try to get to the point. "I might not be able to do all the Daddy things, baby, but I'm still your Daddy and I'll never not be here to comfort you. I need to be able to do that, Asher. *I need to*. Please don't hold back like that."

The words are clumsy and I'm not sure that I'm even making any sense, but Ash rubs his face into my chest and sniffles. "You need your rest. You were *shot*, Charlie. Twice!"

It feels like all I've done since it happened is rest, but that's not what I focus on. "Is... Is that what your nightmare was about?" I don't know why I ask. Ash has always been adamant that he can't remember the details of his dreams, only the way they make him feel. Tonight feels different than all the other times, though.

"That's what they've all been about." His reply is quiet, but it seems to echo in the silence of the room. "Ever since it happened. I can't…" Ash clears his throat. "I know you're okay. Rationally, I know it. But I just keep thinking…I almost lost you. It feels like I just found you and then you were almost gone."

We've spoken about this before and there's nothing either of us can do to resolve these lingering fears. I just hold him closer, kissing the top of his head, and acknowledge the truth in them. "I know, baby. I know. But I'm still here, and I need you to not lock me out, okay? You said it earlier, when the guys were here: we are going to get through this. Together."

I don't know which of us I'm most trying to convince.

Chapter Nineteen — Asher

The first few weeks of Charlie's recovery are rough. He gets easily frustrated when simple tasks evade him because he can't balance without at least one crutch, or when he can't get anywhere as quickly as he'd like. He does his best not to lose his temper, but I've still felt like I've been walking on eggshells around him. When his stitches come out and he's allowed to start using a walking stick instead of crutches, though, a little of his frustration ebbs.

My Little time has been spent much the same way as it was with Ted. I've been getting myself dressed and taking showers instead of baths. I know it has been frustrating Daddy, but I won't risk his recovery.

Daddy and I have been playing games at the dining table —race cars, coloring, even some basic jigsaw puzzles— because he can't kneel on the floor yet. I've been having my bottles and snuggling in bed with him at night, but he needs to sleep on his back and I'm afraid of bumping his leg, so we're sleeping on opposite sides of the king-size mattress. The distance feels like a football field between us.

That said, if I'm being thankful for small mercies, having him with me seems to have staved off the nightmares again, but I desperately miss being wrapped in his arms during the night.

In terms of sex, hand jobs and blow jobs have been the order of the day. Not that either of us is complaining, but I know Charlie misses fucking me as badly as I miss him inside me. The day his physical therapist casually mentions that *certain positions* should be fine if Charlie's careful, we tumble into bed together as soon as we get home from the appointment. I couldn't even bring myself to be embarrassed that the doctor had raised the issue at all. I was too thankful. Too relieved.

Too horny.

We're both hard and aching as we kiss with an intensity that takes my breath away. We have been gentle and cautious up until this point, since Charlie's chest and shoulder are recovering from bullet wounds, but today all bets are off.

I'm giddy as Charlie's hands pull my clothes off roughly. His need makes me burn hotter for him, makes my dick dribble precum and jerk within the confines of my training pants. He's on his back on the mattress and I'm on my knees, leaning over him. His eyes are shining with myriad emotions. I can see his arousal, his love, his relief...and it's all intoxicating.

"Do you want me Big or Little?" I ask him, because honestly, I'm teetering on the edge of either right now. This is the closest we have felt to *us* in a long time, and I want everything with him.

He considers it for a moment, and I can see that he wants it all just as badly as I do. "Big," he eventually decides. His strong hands sweep over the muscles of my back, down to my hips, and tug my undone pants down my thighs, along with my underwear.

I climb off the bed with reluctance and push them the rest of the way down, hopping as my left foot gets caught in my underwear. We both laugh. I pause to remove the last of my clothes and then crawl back over my man. He's trimmed his beard back again to that length that's just a touch longer than stubble and I lean back over him, nuzzling his jaw before our lips reconnect.

Then I carefully unbutton his shirt, helping it over his injured shoulder, and he tugs it off the other side when I'm done. He balls it up and sends it sailing across the room. I shuffle down the mattress and tuck my fingers into the waistband of the sweatpants he's taken to wearing because they are loose fitting and don't put unnecessary pressure on his injury. He plants both feet on the bed, bearing most of his weight on his left leg, and lifts his hips so I can pull the pants and his boxer briefs down and off.

I toss them over the edge of the mattress and then stretch myself out next to him, pressing my naked body against his. This time when we kiss, it's sweeter.

"Hi," I say softly, smiling down at him. He's rolled to face me, resting on his left side, and I gasp as our cocks rub against each other.

"Hey," he responds, equally reverent.

"Did you want to just do this?" I ask him on a whisper, rocking my hips, our precum slicking the connection between us. "Or did you want me to ride you?"

Charlie groans. "Ride me, baby. It's been too long."

Nodding in agreement, I roll away to my bedside table and dig around for the lube in the drawer. I open the lid with a click and grin saucily. "Wanna prep me? Or wanna watch me do it?"

I'm not used to giving him options. He's usually the one who sets the pace and makes the decisions ahead of time. But as he said, it's been a while and he wanted me Big. His equal. His partner in this as much as everything else. To hazard a guess, I think he's in his head about his limitations and I want so desperately to make it all better for him.

"Your ass is mine," he answers in a sexy growl, and I don't need any further encouragement.

With him still propped on his side, I roll to my hands and knees and turn sideways across the bed so he doesn't have to pretzel himself into an awkward angle. I rest forward on my elbows, my ass in the air, and suck in a breath when I feel his lube-covered finger circle my hole. He teases for what feels like forever, circling the rim, barely pressing in. He smacks my ass when I try rocking back into him. The *zing* of it goes straight to my cock and I smother a groan.

I'm not usually big on impact play. Before Charlie was injured, we tried a couple of spanking scenes, but they felt awkward to me. Maybe I was too Little for it at the time, though, because the sting and the unexpected heat of his palm on my skin light me up from the inside this time.

Charlie definitely notices. "That's new," he observes, smoothing his hand over the spot he smacked.

"Uh-huh," I answer. Words are hard right now. "Explore later. Fuck me now."

With a chuckle, his finger probes gently at my hole again. "So impatient," he says accusingly, but I know that he's just as desperate for this as I am. Still, it's the first genuine glimpse of my playful Daddy that I've seen in weeks, and I go with it.

"Please Daddy," I whine, and I rock back against his probing digit again, forgetting my promise to remain Big. "Make me feel good."

"I'll get you there, baby." His voice is suddenly tight and gruff, and now I wonder if him asking me to stay Big was for other reasons. I know he hasn't felt whole in his Daddy role lately. I make a note to discuss it with him later.

Right now, sex.

"*Charlie*," I plead while I grind against his teasing finger, then I moan loudly as he gives me exactly what I've been begging for. He takes it slowly, twisting that one thick digit before eventually adding more lube and a second finger. It feels like he spends hours this way, too, scissoring them and stretching me while I babble and demand more. Crooking them, he grazes my prostate and I buck against him, and my cock jerks, precum practically pouring from me. "*Now*, Charlie, please."

He swats my ass again, taking me by surprise and I thrust backward, fucking myself on his fingers. He adds a third, no longer slow and teasing, just stretching and fucking me with his fingers until he deems me ready. When he pulls his fingers out, I whimper, but then I remember that I get to ride him, and I push up onto my knees with haste.

I turn to face Charlie, who has rolled onto his back and has drizzled more lube into his fist, stroking it over his impressive length. He looks impossibly hard, the head of his cock an angry red, and I push his hand away so I can gingerly straddle his hips.

I lock my gaze on his, the blue of his eyes so dark that I almost forget what I wanted to say. "You safe word out if I hurt your leg," I demand in a tone that brooks no argument. "Understood?" He might be the Daddy, but his safety and recovery is far more important to me than orgasms and our usual roles.

With a warm, understanding look on his handsome face, Charlie nods and grips my thighs. "I promise."

Nothing more needs to be said. I reach beneath me to guide him to my entrance and then slowly bear down, watching Charlie's face the entire time. He steels his jaw and slides his eyes shut when he bottoms out, exhaling heavily.

"Fuck, I've missed you, baby," he murmurs, so quietly that I almost don't hear it. "Missed being inside you."

"Me too," I whisper back, a knot of emotion in my throat.

Starting to move, I force myself to be slow and careful. Charlie's hand wraps around my shaft, still slick from the lube, and he starts rocking his hips and fucking up into me, setting a faster pace that I happily fall into.

I bend forward and tangle my hand in the hair at the back of his head, kissing him deeply and desperately. With the change in angle and the natural curve of his cock, he brushes my prostate with every quick thrust. I'm seeing stars, my balls drawing tight, electricity zapping along the base of my spine.

"I'm close," I warn him, my forehead pressed to his. "Charlie, I..."

He stares into my eyes. Beyond the fire in them, there's joy and intensity and that glimmer of relief again. "Come for me, baby."

And I do. I still my hips, my cock jerking in his hold as I spill over his fist and abdomen. Then he's groaning and I feel the warmth of his release inside me. We're both panting and I wince as I climb off him as cautiously as possible. I bend down for another kiss, back to languorous but with an edge of neediness that neither of us has completely shed yet.

"I'll just grab a washcloth," I tell him when I pull back, feeling the not-exactly-pleasant sensation of cum trickling out of me.

Charlie shakes his head and pushes himself up, swinging his legs over the edge of the bed. "Shower with me," he says, and I bite back my surprise. He's been forced to use a shower chair and hasn't wanted me to see him in it, even though it had given me some delightfully naughty ideas.

"I'd like that a lot," I answer. I hook my arm around his waist, and he leans on me instead of a crutch as we head into the ensuite.

Under the hot spray, we put some of my ideas into action after all. It's such a relief to see him return to his playful self that I find myself slipping back into my Little headspace when we finally make our way back to bed, cleaned off and satiated.

Once I'm there, cocooned in Daddy's sleepy-time hold for the first time in what feels like forever, the tension of the last few weeks melts away.

We're going to be okay, I realize before sleep claims me. We've gone through a lot together in such a short amount of time and come out stronger for it. And even though I've thought it before, I can't help but acknowledge just how lucky I am to have him with me. My Daddy. My partner. The answer to all my unspoken prayers. The man who opened his home to me when I was a broken shell of myself. The man who not only accepted the things I was most ashamed of but also celebrated them with me.

We still have a lot to discuss —numerous issues that we will have to face together, like his career and his obvious feelings of self-recrimination— but I know it's all going to be okay.

Daddy's got this, and I've got him.

Epilogue — Charlie

~ ⚬∾⚬ ~

It's been just over a year since I got shot. Life has returned to some semblance of normal, and we're happy and thriving. Ash is still in therapy, but he's managing his anxiety with so much grace and strength that it blows me away. He even convinced me to see a therapist over my lingering frustration at the sudden end to my career, and I have to admit that it has helped a lot.

Being forced to retire threw me for a loop at first. I'd known it was possible, but I'd remained optimistic. Unfortunately, I still have a mild limp from the bullet I took to my thigh, and I didn't pass the medical to return to my usual duties. I did receive a disability retirement pension, though, having been injured in the line of duty. The backup plans I originally considered are still floating around in my mind, even if I feel like they're a pipe dream for the time being.

I want to do something for the kink community, particularly the age-regression subset. I'd like to potentially work in conjunction with The Grove to create a space that's a haven for at-risk people...like Asher was.

I want to know if it's possible to create a safe house for people in the kink community to stay in if they find themselves suddenly homeless. It happens more frequently than I'd imagined: apparently even Matt experienced this before we met him. Ash found that news particularly distressing, despite Matt being settled and safe now. So, ideally, this would be my main priority.

But I'd like to expand the idea further. To create a safe, welcoming, judgment-free zone where people interested in the BDSM lifestyle can meet, learn, and network with other members of the community without feeling like a kink night-club or a public munch are their only options.

Ted is helping me sort through the legalities of the sort of things I want to achieve, but it's all hypothetical at the moment. Ash has also contributed some ideas of his own, and his perspective has me rethinking some of the plans.

But that's all still in the air. It's something to keep me busy while my beautiful man continues to find his footing at work and in study, and I'm content to let it happen slowly.

So today finds us hosting another get-together with our friends, and it's a far cry from the first time. Sadly, Spence and Emma broke up, so we're minus one Little, but everyone's seated around the large outdoor table laughing, drinking and eating, and it feels perfect. Ash is over by the grill, turning burgers and teasing Matt; Ted is regaling Chance, Josh, and Max with his plans to renovate the huge house he just bought; and Spence is at my side, debating whether he should get a pet to fill the void Emma left behind.

"Get a cat," I tell him, and from across the deck Ash turns to me with a grin.

"Kitty?" He bounces on his heels. "Oh, Daddy, please can we get a kitty?"

Spence laughs and nudges me. "Now you've done it."

"We're not getting a cat," I argue back playfully. "You're enough of a handful on your own."

"Pfft" —he waves the spatula in the air in front of him— "you love me and you know it."

I do. Everyone here knows just how in love I am with him. In fact, once the burgers are done and we're all seated and comfortable, I've got plans to formalize that. But, for now, while he's sassing me, I have to sass back.

Tapping my chin, I muse with exaggeration, "Hmm, do I?"

Ash gives me the finger and turns back to the grill, but he's wiggling his butt, so I know the cold shoulder is for show.

Smirking at his back, I put on my Daddy voice knowing just what it does to him. "Do you want a spanking, Asher?"

The look he throws me over his shoulder is smoldering. "Always, Daddy."

He really has come out of his shell and embraced our lifestyle. He no longer blushes at the chuckles and whistles from our friends, and when Chance declares that I'm letting my boy get bratty, Ash scowls and brandishes the spatula in Chance's direction. "For that, you're not getting dessert, Uncle Chance."

I know that our dynamic isn't exactly usual for Daddy/Little roles. I don't care about Ash's potty mouth or his attitude when he's Big, and he doesn't rely on me to resolve all his problems or do things for him. He likes to feel independent as an adult, and I enjoy having a lover and boyfriend to hang out with, even if I do like doting on him then, too.

But at the same time, things change when he slips into his Little space, which now tends to happen on a whim. We don't really plan for it, outside of the few dedicated hours after work where Ash needs the relaxation, and it blends effortlessly into our lives.

This is exactly the balance that I was looking for and thought was a myth. In my experience, not many littles have done well without strict routines; my exes wanted me to make all their life decisions for them and wanted to be Little more often than not. As much as I had liked taking care of them, it had wound up putting too much stress on me, especially when my job had thrown wrenches in the works.

I'd almost given up hope that there was a Little out there who would be okay with a more fluid situation — with more give and take, and more flexibility. I certainly hadn't expected to meet him outside of the kink community.

It's funny how life works sometimes.

When there's a spread of food on the table, Ash finally drops into my lap and snuggles into me with all sense of his bratty, bigger self gone. Once again I muse on my luck. I still can't believe that this gorgeous boy is mine. It really does look like I've found my unicorn, and the sensation of just how perfect we are together settles over me. It feels good and *right*. He makes me whole.

That thought spurs another on:

It's go time.

When I first planned this moment, I thought I'd be nervous. But, looking at Ash, seeing the way he fits so perfectly into my life and my world, I'm settled and confident. This is a formality and a confirmation of what we mean to each other. He's not going to reject me, not after everything we've been through together already.

Nudging him to sit up, I reach into my jacket pocket and

pull out the ring box I'd stuffed in there earlier. As I hold it out in front of him, I'm dimly aware of the sounds around us stopping, the chatter and laughter from our friends turning to stunned silence, the clink of cutlery cut off.

"Wha—Charlie?" Ash's eyes are wide with surprise, but there's excitement and joy and love simmering beneath the expression. While I would have happily proposed to him in his Little space, I find relief in him coming back out of it to meet me as his partner again.

I had a whole speech prepared. Words about how much he means to me. The story of us consolidated into thirty seconds of justification for this moment. But I don't say any of it. I don't have to. He knows it all and then some. What I do say is "Little lamb, will you marry me?" and it's enough.

Asher squeals and shouts a very emphatic "Yes!" before he slams his lips to mine, and our friends hoot and holler. They start congratulating us as I slide the simple platinum band onto Ash's ring finger, and he holds it up with pride.

"Mom's going to kill you for not inviting them for this," Josh says with a laugh, from his spot between Max and Matt.

I roll my eyes. "If we could get away with eloping, I'd do that, too."

Holding his beer bottle up in the air in a salute, Josh tilts it forward and nods. "Fair. I just hope you realize what you're setting yourself up for."

I know he means Mom's enthusiasm for wedding planning (Maisy's dramatic ordeal still makes me shudder), but my brain goes elsewhere. Pinning Ash with a soft smile, I say, "A lifetime of happiness, I hope."

The guys cheer again and glasses clink, but Ash and I disappear into our own little bubble for a moment.

Epilogue – Charlie

He kisses my lips tenderly before he pulls back, those plump lips curving upward in a gentle smile that mirrors mine. His hazel eyes are so full of love and assurance as he replies, "A lifetime of happiness for sure."

The End.

*** * *

Thank you so much for reading *Asher's Answer.* I genuinely hope you liked it as much as I enjoyed writing it. I'd love it if you could leave a review on Goodreads and/or your favorite online retailer - reviews not only tell the algorithms that our books deserve attention, but honest feedback also encourages and inspires me to keep writing. Even a star rating helps, and I greatly appreciate you taking the time to help.

Speaking of my writing…if you liked meeting the crew in Book 1 of *Littles and Lace*, keep turning the pages for a sneak peek of Book 2 titled *Matteo's Mettle*!

Also, if you'd like to read a zero-angst, super fluffy novella which functions as an extended epilogue for *Asher's Answer*, subscribe to my newsletter via:

https://annasparrows.com/newsletter-subscription/

For updates, release dates, competitions and more, follow me on Facebook. The link is in the 'About The Author' page after the sneak peek.

Matteo's Mettle – Sneak Peek

Chapter One – Matteo

Just under two years ago, I reached the lowest point of my life. I'd turned forty-three and my Daddy, a man I'd been with for almost a decade, sat me down and told me that our relationship wasn't working for him anymore. Heartbroken didn't quite cover how I felt.

I'd given that man the prime years of my life and he was ending it without any warning. Hell, the night before had been just like any other. We'd had sex, exchanging words of affection as always, and then we'd gone through my Little night-time routine. Bath time, diapering, a bedtime story, and a bottle as I snuggled up alongside him. It was the same routine he had set when we first got together, when I was new to the world of BDSM and kink play.

I was a late bloomer, I guess. Imagine being in your thirties and discovering sides of yourself you'd never known were there.

Ladies and gentlemen, I give you Matteo Brightman: dense

as fuck.

So, yeah. Daddy had sat me down three weeks after my forty-third birthday and ended our relationship. Just like that. He'd been clinical and impassive about it, hinting that I wasn't the kind of Little he wanted anymore. Not as I inched toward my mid-forties. Not with my bulky build and tattooed skin – changes I'd made over the course of the decade which he had been wholly supportive of at the time. I understood. I was graying at the temples, and I was physically too big and 'masculine' to fit the 'Little' stereotype. Still, surely ten years of togetherness should have meant *something* to him?

Spoiler alert: it did not.

Unfortunately, nothing I said moved him. He hadn't reacted to my tears, either. That had cemented the whole breakup for me. If Daddy was impassive in the face of my tears, things really were over.

The only friends I had were all his to start with; people in the lifestyle he had introduced me to. None had been willing to 'get in the middle' of our breakup by allowing me to couch surf. I spent one night at a colleague's place, then called my dad and arranged to move back in with him until I could sort my shit out. The only issue with that was moving halfway across the country.

I'd seen it as a win, though. A fresh start away from the reminder of my shattered heart and ruined life. As an electrical engineer, finding another job near Dad's place wasn't too difficult. Starting my whole life over again at forty-three? That turned out to be much harder.

Especially when Dad died from a sudden heart attack three months after I moved in.

The only thing that consoled me in my grief was that I'd

had those three months with him. If Trent -my Daddy- hadn't dumped me when he did, I would never have moved back home. In some ways, I was glad that the end of my relationship had given me those last few months with my father.

Following Dad's death, I threw myself into work. I'd inherited his house -the one I'd grown up in- and, when I wasn't working, I was doing small renovations. It was both rewarding and necessary. I had needed to make the space my own as part of my grieving process. Close to three months following his death, I discovered The Grove.

It had happened by complete accident. One of the guys at work had mentioned it under his breath. The Grove had hired our company to update their high-tech monitoring systems and the teams working on the project had all had to sign hefty non-disclosure agreements. Craig -a younger, kind of arrogant engineer- had been in the employee break room with another member of their team, muttering derisively about 'fetishists' and 'kinky freaks' under his breath while I'd been waiting for my lunch to heat up in the microwave.

My ears had perked up immediately, my stomach swooping with hope.

It had been six months since I had truly indulged my kinky urges. Before Dad had died, I'd tried a couple of BDSM clubs in the city, but my experiences had not been positive. It turned out Trent wasn't the only Daddy who thought I was too big and too old to be a Little. I'd been beginning to wonder if maybe they were right.

Unfortunately, though, my heart -and dick- weren't giving up on my interests or my needs. This was who I was always going to be. A Little. I had an inherent need to be cherished and cared for and, yeah, *babied*…for lack of a better word.

I loved having a Daddy to play with me, bathe me, diaper and dress me. I loved having my decisions -when I wasn't at work- taken care of for me. My food chosen and cut up for me, my entertainment arranged by someone else. It made the maelstrom of stressful thoughts in my head cease.

And the fact that I enjoyed the sexual aspect of the Daddy/Little boy dynamic? That was the cherry on top.

Well, it had been in my thirties. Before I'd bulked up. Trent had been a gym rat and, with nothing else to do but follow along, I'd discovered that I enjoyed weight training, too. He had supported it. Had even said that he loved how big and strong I was becoming. He'd always had a thing for buff men. He hadn't ever complained that it made it more difficult to find onesies and Little clothes that fit properly, or that I was beginning to look ridiculous wearing them.

Not until he dumped my sorry ass, anyway.

So heading back out into the community -into a new city where I didn't know anybody else involved the lifestyle- was rough. Most Daddies aren't into a boy who could bench press them, or who 'looks like a sad reject from *Sons of Anarchy*' if the guy I'd met at my first club's assessment was to be believed. I felt lost and alone, and indulging in cartoons at home in a diaper I'd put on myself was a cold comfort at best.

Would The Grove be able to offer anything that the other clubs had not? It had sounded like it was a more professional establishment, if the NDAs our company had needed to sign were any indication, but I was wary.

Still, I reached out to them anyway. Meg -one of the three women who manned the front desk- had been so sweet and helpful. She'd answered all my questions and invited me to the next dedicated Littles' Night where they would open the doors to non-members (after a vetting process) to check out the space and interact with other caregivers and littles. The club would also organize a variety of fun activities for the evening as part of the themed event. I signed up on the spot.

Even though I didn't meet any potential Daddies that night, I made a connection with another buff Little. Josh Walker. When I'm Little, I'm painfully shy, but that hadn't stopped the guy from plopping down beside me at the pottery station and chatting my ears off. By the end of the night, I'd left with a smile on my face and a new friend's contact number in my phone.

However, while Josh introduced me to his brother and his friends in kink community, I still longed to find a Daddy of my own.

Hell, eighteen months on from that and I'm still lonely as fuck.

Maybe it's just time to hang up my onesies and settle for a vanilla relationship. As much as I hate that idea, I hate the idea of being alone forever even more.

"Earth to Matt," my friend and fellow Little, Ash, waves his hand in my face. I'm at the house he shares with his Daddy and fiancé, Charlie, and we've been playing with blocks in the lounge room.

These playdates have been happening ever since Josh introduced me to the guys. Charlie also happens to be Josh's older brother, and they have a close-knit social circle of kinky friends. Even now, I'm still amazed that they invited me to be a part of it.

Charlie -a former cop- has also been kind enough to be my caretaker during these playdates. He's a decade my junior, but he's got Daddy vibes for days. To be honest, I've always been a little envious of Asher -who is in his early twenties, has a slender, athletic frame and guileless wide hazel eyes- for his luck finding such a perfect Daddy. Not that I'd be Charlie's type, obviously, but I badly want what they share together.

I don't allow myself to regress too far with Charlie. I don't need him changing me or giving me a bottle. But he does cut up my meals while I'm here and cuddle me on the couch when the three of us enjoy story time. It's the most bitter-sweet feeling: I get a taste of the life I want, but I also know this isn't mine to really enjoy.

"Matt?"

I give myself a little shake at Ash's repetition of my name. Biting my lip, I offer him a sheepish grin. "Sorry. I was just thinking."

Ash frowns and cocks his head. "About?"

He's not overly Little today, either. He tends to be more fluid in the way he drifts in between his Little and Big personas, but it is unusual that he's not letting go during our playdate. I feel a bit guilty, because I can see his concern for me written all over his expressive face and I'm guessing that's what's keeping him from losing himself.

Great. Now I'm bringing him down, too.

With a sigh, I drop the orange cylindrical block I've been fiddling with for the last few minutes and shrug. "Nothing important."

His eyes narrow. After observing me for a moment longer, he looks up and over my shoulder, where Charlie's lounging on the couch with a book. "Charlie, we're done here," he declares without any trace of his Little self in his words and unfolds himself from his cross-legged position with a grace I wish I could emulate. He climbs to his feet and dusts imaginary lint off his play shorts. Then he offers me his hand.

Taking it, I groan as he helps pull me to my feet where I tower over him. My knees and back protest painfully. Another sign that maybe I really am getting too old for this. I can't quite school my face in time, and I know that Ash catches the flicker of mourning I just felt.

Still eyeing me carefully, he says, "Let's get changed, then grab a beer."

It's more a demand than a suggestion.

Nodding, I head toward the guest bathroom upstairs where I left my adult clothes and can hear Charlie and Ash murmuring quietly as I go. When I meet them back in the kitchen a handful of minutes later, their combined worry for me is almost palpable.

I offer Charlie a grateful "Thank you" when he hands me a bottle of pale ale, the cap already popped.

Ash and Charlie let me take a deep draw from the amber bottle before Charlie asks, "What's going on?"

I look back across the kitchen island at him. He's got his arm wrapped around Ash, but his eyes are narrowed on me. He and I are close in height and build, where Ash is a handful of inches shorter. Charlie's got a neatly trimmed, thick dark beard and startlingly blue eyes. He's a handsome man, and Ash is equally pretty. Nestled together as they are, they make a beautiful couple and my heart aches with jealousy and loneliness even more.

Get it together, Brightman.

"It's nothing," I try to brush off the question, but these guys know me better than that by now.

While we might only have been in each other's lives for eighteen months or so, I like to think that we've gotten close.

I would say that I have connected more with them and Josh than with the other guys in our social circle. It comes from spending so much time on playdates with Ash, I suppose.

As expected, Charlie scoffs. *"Matteo,"* he goes full Daddy, all stern and expectant.

He's not my Daddy, but with all the time we've spent together with him as my proxy caretaker, I'm still wired to respond. "Ugh, that's a sneaky tactic, asshole," I tilt the neck of my beer bottle at him in accusation and he raises an eyebrow, not wavering. *Damn it.* Swallowing roughly, I look up at the ceiling. "I'm just all up in my head right now. I'm feeling…" *Lost. Alone. Hopeless. Broken. Pathetic.* "…tired."

Charlie's expression remains neutral as he continues to observe me in silence. I pick at the label on my beer bottle, averting my eyes under his scrutiny. But it's not him who speaks next. It's Ash.

"You're lonely."

Even though they're delivered softly and with obvious compassion, the words seem to echo around us and I flinch. My shoulders lift and droop in a shrug, and now I really can't meet either of their gazes.

Running my finger through the condensation dripping down the bottle in my hand, I try to brush the whole thing off. "It's just…I don't know…like a midlife crisis. It's stupid."

I'll be turning forty-five in another week, and I assume that's been a trigger for these feelings. Another birthday to spend on my own. Another sign that I'm aging out of the lifestyle I enjoy so deeply.

Forty-five. Fucking hell.

"It's not stupid," Ash argues, slipping out of Charlie's embrace and circling the kitchen island. He wraps one of his arms around me and pulls my head down to his shoulder. I hate myself for soaking up the affection like a sponge. "Have you thought about-"

"I'm not going back again." This I am firm on. "Every time I go, it's the same shit. I can't..."

Fuck it.

My voice breaks, and my throat clogs with tears. The truth is, I can't handle constantly being told what I know deep in my bones: I'm not a desirable Little. And it stings all the more that I'm about to have this breakdown on the shoulder of a *perfect* Little. I shouldn't resent him for his youth or his slimmer frame, but some part of me does, and that makes me feel like an incredibly shitty friend on top of everything else.

It's bad enough that I'm jealous of the relationship he and Charlie have, but being envious of his appearance? What am I, twelve? I give myself a mental shake and go back to the issue at hand.

The clientele at The Grove are certainly of a higher caliber than at the other clubs in the city, but the rejection there has been hurtful all the same. Even at The Grove, or in the online groups Josh and Ash suggested I join, the Daddies are looking for cute, sweet littles. *Littles like Ash.* They're usually kind about turning down my advances, but I don't have it in me to try anymore.

"I'm done." I say into the silence that has once again descended. My voice is shaky, and I can feel my heart breaking, already grieving the life I've decided to say goodbye to. "I'm giving up age play."

Ash gasps, and out of the corner of my eye I watch his hand fly to his mouth.

Across the kitchen island, Charlie's voice is low and equally surprised. "Matt…"

Forcing myself to look up, I steel my jaw. Looking between them, I shake my head. "I've been thinking about this for a while. I need to walk away from it."

I'm surprised by how convinced I sound to my own ears.

If only my heart would get with the program.

About the Author

I've been writing* for as long as I can remember. I started with silly short stories as a kid, moved on to fanfiction in my teens (and still write it now), and am also a published MF romance author under a second pen name.

I have been an avid reader of MM romance my whole life. (Ask me about my beginnings with *Buffy* fanfic, haha.) I wrote a sweet and kinky MM romance novel in 2022 and the reader response changed my life. From there, I knew I had found my niche.

And thus Anna Sparrows was born.

*All of my writing is 100% my own. No part of it is generated by Artificial Intelligence (AI) software of any kind. Yes, that means that it's sometimes flawed, but I'm okay with that.

You can connect with me on:
🌐 https://annasparrows.com
f https://www.facebook.com/AnnaSparrowsAuthor

Subscribe to my newsletter:
✉ https://annasparrows.com/newsletter-subscription

Also by Anna Sparrows

I write ridiculously sweet & steamy MM romance with guaranteed HEAs…and sometimes with a side of kink.

Littles & Lace series

The Littles & Lace series is an MM Age Play series, following a group of like-minded friends in the BDSM community. You'll find mild ABDL, light Pet Play, Femme Play and more here.

Book 1: Asher's Answer

Book 2: Matteo's Mettle

Book 3: Ted's Temerity

Book 4: Spencer's Satisfaction

Book 5: Chance's Choice

Book 6: Josh's Jackpot

Dads & Adages series
Visit Australia's sunny Gold Coast where an assortment of single dads find love and even learn a few life lessons along the way.

Book 1: Where There's A Will

Book 2: You Don't Know Jack

Book 3: A Match Made In Evan (release TBA)

Shifters Sanctuary Series
In a world where alphas are thought to be extinct, a number of 'human' men are about to have their worlds rocked.

Book 1: His Alpha Unlocked

Book 2: His Prodigal Alpha (release TBA)